D0891587

ICE

THE ARAB LIST

SONALLAH IBRAHIM

I C E

Translated by
Margaret Litvin

LONDON NEW YORK CALCUTTA

Series Editor
Hosam Aboul-Ela

Seagull Books, 2019

First published in Arabic as *Al-Jalid* by Sonallah Ibrahim

© Sonallah Ibrahim, 2011

First published in English by Seagull Books, 2019

English translation and Afterword © Margaret Litvin, 2019

ISBN   978 0 8574 2 650 5

British Library Cataloguing-in-Publication Data

A catalogue record for this book is available from
the British Library

Typeset by Seagull Books, Calcutta, India
Printed and bound by Hyam Enterprises, Calcutta, India

contents

1

The *komendantsha* who ran our *obshchezhitie*, the dorm, appeared around noon. First her round, frowning face in its frame of grey hair. Then her fat body, filling our doorway. She would put another student in with us, a Russian, she said. I told her the room had only three beds, but she pointed to a disassembled frame atop the wardrobe. I said, 'I'm thirty-five years old. I can't stand crowding and noise, and besides, I'm supposed to have a private room like the other graduate students.' She looked at me for a moment, perhaps taking the measure of my slight frame: Did I really deserve a whole room to myself? She said, '*Tovarish* Shukri, *ladno*. Fine. We'll keep it just the three of you.'

When she was gone, Mario the Brazilian straightened the 1973 calendar on the wall near the door. He was slim, about my height, with narrow, nervous eyes, wearing an embroidered wool shirt and jeans. He said, twisting his earring, 'They want to put a Russian student in with the foreigners so he can report on them.' Our roommate Jalaleddinov, a tall young man with Asian features from the Kirghiz Soviet Socialist Republic, spoke up as if to deflect suspicion from himself: 'Well. There's nothing worth reporting.'

I put on my overcoat, put a wool *shapka* on my head, wrapped a scarf around my neck and pulled on my fur-lined boots, the ones with thick soles for walking on ice. I checked for my gloves in my pocket, walked down the clean stairs to the ground floor, waved to the *dezhurnaya* minding the door and left the *obshchezhitie*. The sun had disappeared, and I was assailed by the new-fallen snow and the cold air. My nose began to run; I pulled the flaps of my *shapka* over my ears and put on my gloves. I walked carefully on the snow. The glass front of the *magazin* was piled, like in all the stores, with pyramids of evaporated milk cans and nothing else. Over its top was stretched a cloth banner: 'We Are Fulfilling the Plan. Forward Towards Communism.' At the entrance was a small group of drunks. One of them held two fingers together on his jacket sleeve, signalling he needed two more takers to split a half-litre bottle of vodka.

Choosing what to buy was no challenge; the selection was limited. I stood in the queue at the counter looking at the picture of Brezhnev on the wall. One of the white-coated saleswomen disappeared. Two others were absorbed in a long conversation. I was given a receipt for what I wanted. Then I moved over to another queue to pay. The saleswoman added up my purchases on a wooden abacus: 310 kopeks' worth of eggs, 30 of *kefir*, cultured milk, 463 of vodka and 80 of bread. I paid and collected my receipt, then moved to the third queue to receive my purchases.

I was about to pick up the bread with my bare hand, but the worker brushed me away roughly and grabbed the loaf with metal tongs. I left the shop and stopped to watch a policeman who had pushed a man to the wall and was beating him savagely. Then he threw him in a police car.

I passed an old woman in a white overcoat and black boots with a box of stuffed pancakes called *piroshki*. She opened the box to sell one and recoiled from the scorching steam. I walked to the cigarette kiosk run by a white-haired old man. When I got there, I was surprised to see the window closed and the man engrossed in studying some cigarette boxes laid out in his hand. He did this extremely slowly, his hand trembling. He looked over the contents again, counted the money he had accumulated, then searched for something. Meanwhile a queue formed behind me. I began hopping on my feet to warm them. I heard someone say the temperature was ten below zero.

'The old guy's looking for his dick,' someone else said.

'Did he find it?' a third person asked.

'Of course not.'

The white-haired man began arranging new brands of cigarettes behind the glass and labelling the prices. When one of the labels slipped, he adjusted it slowly. Finally he opened the window. I bought a box of TU-144 cigarettes and returned to the *obshchezhitie*.

My hands were frozen. I hurried to the ground-floor bathroom to run cold water over them as I had been advised. I felt pain in my fingers as the heat reached them.

I went to the *komendantsha* to get some clean sheets. On my way up the stairs, I almost collided with Vera, the perpetually miniskirted Jewish girl. I went up to my room on the fourth floor; there was no one there. I cooked three eggs in the floor's shared kitchen and washed them down with a cup of good tea—*Gruzinski*, from the Georgian SSR. I lit a cigarette and took a strong drag; the filter came off in my mouth. I felt sleepy, so I stretched out on my bed in the right-hand corner, opposite Mario's. Jalaleddinov's bed was pushed next to the foot of mine in a straight line, with his head to my feet.

Jalaleddinov woke me up when he came in. He leant on the small wooden dresser and said, '*Tovarish* Shukri, I know Egyptians are generous. I'm a Muslim like you, and I need a favour.'

'Go ahead.'

He told me he had a Russian girlfriend in his village whom he wanted to marry, but she had no residence permit for Moscow, so could he bring her to live with us?

'How will she sleep?' I asked.

'In my bed, and we'll make a curtain around us.'

'Did you ask Mario?'

'Yes, he agreed.'

I nodded my agreement; his face lit up, and he began packing his bag to go to the village to bring his girlfriend.

Jalaleddinov told me Mario was leaving that night for Leningrad. I went down to the ground floor and put 2 kopeks into the payphone. I dialled Madeleine at the Institute of Languages. I waited until they called her to the phone, then invited her to come over the next day.

'And Mario? I don't want him to see me.'

'He'll be away. He's leaving on a trip tonight.'

2

I shaved with a crude Soviet razor, wondering at the Soviets: They build rockets and they haven't managed or can't be bothered to build a decent razor blade. I took some clean clothes and went down to the public bathroom on the ground floor for a hot shower. I came back to my room and hung my towel on the hot radiator to dry. At five o'clock Madeleine came upstairs, having left her ID card with the guard. She was Brazilian, in her mid-twenties; a fine-boned brunette, slightly buck-toothed. I had met her and Mario in Russian class. I gave her a hug and brought in a pot of tea from the kitchen. With excitement she showed me what she had brought: a record by Roberto Carlos, the Brazilian singer, and a spray bottle of cologne as a gift for me. We put the record on the portable player, and locked the door. I took off my trousers and sat down in my woollen long underwear; she took off her thick burgundy tights. I felt her thighs: wet. Usually I asked her about the safe time of the month, and we would count the days since her last period. But this time I forgot, and didn't think about it till I was inside her. I asked her; she wasn't offended. She always gave in to me, saying she trusted me and that I knew everything. She tried to kiss me, but

I pulled away. I didn't like her lips. I avoided her breasts, too, since she never felt anything when I fondled them. She said after a moment, 'Beat me.' I didn't; that wasn't my thing, either.

After we finished, the pain in my penis recurred, but she sighed contentedly and said, 'It doesn't hurt any more like it did with my boyfriend Hermann. His penis was so thick. Maybe I've stretched out with practice.'

3

There was a knock at the door. I asked, '*Kto tam?*—Who is it?' I opened it for Hans the handsome German. About thirty, taller than me, with his soft blonde hair falling over his forehead and parted in the middle, and his fleshy lips. He would come from East Germany a few times a year to meet with his thesis supervisor. He greeted me: '*Privet.*' He said he had two Russian students with him, girls who lived on the fifth floor. He asked me to come over because both Farid and Hamid, his two Syrian roommates, were out.

I carried my record player and an Arabic LP to his room. The two girls were in their early twenties. Zoya, slim, my height or a little taller, with a childlike face, blue eyes, short blonde hair and small breasts, married to a conscript doing his military service far away. And the other one, also blonde, named Talia, with plain features, nothing special.

The room had two beds facing each other; a third stood behind a wooden wardrobe that took up the width of the room near the door. I put the record player on a desk under the window between the two beds and put on the Arabic record. The girls listened in silence until Talia said, 'Don't you have any dance music?' I went to my room and brought three Western LPs—modern music. I put one of them on, and Zoya clapped her hands.

Hans brought out vodka and a piece of cheese and half-frozen bread. He poured for us and drained his glass at once, saying, '*Za zdorovie*—to health.' I raised my glass to my lips and took a sip. Zoya said, 'Not like that, you have to drink your glass all at once.'

'I don't want to get drunk,' I said.

'I'll teach you how to stay sober. First, smell the vodka, then take a sip and leave it in your mouth for a second, then swallow it and shoot the rest of it all at once and eat something right away.'

I drained my glass according to her instructions, then took a slice of bread. She said her father used to drink nothing but concentrated alcohol and refused to mix it with water or anything; and, to make sure it was pure, he would fill a glass and light it on fire, and only if it ignited would he snuff out the flames and drink it. Talia changed the subject: 'There are only a few places where you can get fresh soft white bread. Kutuzovsky Prospekt close to Brezhnev's house, and the shop in Gorky Street, and the Arts Cinema in Arbat.' When I declined a second glass, Hans said, 'We have to finish the bottle. There's no way to close it once it's open.' Zoya moved a lock of hair that had fallen across her eyes and tucked it behind her ear. She asked me what would become of the Arab lands that Israel had occupied. I said they would only be liberated if the Arab governments changed.

'But don't some of them believe in socialism?'

'That's what they claim.'

I told her about the War of Attrition we had been waging against the occupation for years.

Zoya was sitting next to Hans on his bed, and Talia stretched out across the facing bed, leaning her head against the wall. I sat on the only armchair, beside the table. Talia asked me if I had fought in the war. I said I had been a conscript in a military office far from the front; after returning to teach at my university I was awarded a scholarship for a cultural exchange programme with the Soviet Union. Zoya suggested turning out the light. We lit some candles. Hans pulled her up for a dance, and she submitted to his embrace. I did not move from my place. My eyes were glued to their faces and her bare legs. Talia gave me a silent look. Then she asked me about the woman question in Egypt. I said the Egyptian woman's situation had improved greatly since the revolution: she had taken off the face veil and begun to enter many occupations—these days she could even work as a bus conductor. Soon Talia got up: 'I'm going. I need to study.' She asked her friend, 'Aren't you coming with me?' Hans said, 'Let her stay a little.' Talia left, and the two of them kept dancing. After a while, they sat down on the bed. We all sat in silence. Eventually I excused myself, picked up my record player and LPs and went to my room.

4

There was no hot water to shave with, and I mumbled in irritation, Lord, oh Lord. I came upon a single egg and took it to the kitchen, putting it to boil on the stove. I returned to the room, singing 'This Egg Is My Egg' to the triumphant tune of the old 1956 War song:

This land is my land, *da da dum*,
Where my father fell in battle.
And here my father told us:
Tear our enemies to shreds.

I translated the words into English for Mario, which he understood well. He laughed and asked, 'What are you doing tonight?'

'I haven't decided yet—you?'

He said he would spend the evening with the Brazilians.

'Madeleine?'

'Yeah, and her friend Isadora and some others.'

Isadora was dark, exploding with femininity, with proud African features. She fascinated me, but I was too timid, so I went after her friend Madeleine instead. Isadora, in turn, got together with a Brazilian guy named

Hector. Handsome and athletic, he seemed to be from one of those bourgeois families destined to succeed at sports and social activities.

Mario left for the Institute. I went to the window and watched the snow falling; I pulled up the glass windowpane. Behind it was another glass pane, with a little slit for ventilation, and between them a space that served as a refrigerator for our butter, cheese and *kolbasa*, salami. I took out the butter and put it on the table next to the black bread and the cheese and jam. I went to the kitchen and boiled water for tea and brought it back to the room. As usual, Farid knocked on my door. He was short and chubby, with a loud voice and a thick moustache. He had taken to starting his day by visiting me and sharing my breakfast. We sat down to eat as he chattered. He told me about Hamid, who would finish his studies this year, and about Hans, and their nonstop female conquests. As usual I felt his voice burning my ears; a sinking feeling seized me, and I wished he would leave.

5

I set out for the Institute of Contemporary History, on foot despite the snow. The streets were full of remnants of small green Christmas trees, and the balconies of blocks of flats were strung with coloured lights and slogans: 'The Party and the People Are One'; 'Power to Labour'; 'Long Live the Soviet People, Building Communism.' I was stopped at the entrance by a guard in a black uniform decorated with brass buttons. I showed him my ID card and pushed open the glass door. I saw, looking down at me, the face of Lenin carved into the woodwork and above it a banner announcing: 'Forward Towards the Victory of Communism.' I took off my overcoat and put it in the cloakroom along with my scarf and *shapka*.

I went to Russian class. The teacher was in her midthirties and wore a short skirt over white tights. Afterwards I ate lunch in the cafeteria: a piece of cabbage that smelt like dishwater, black bread, a goulash with scraps of meat in it, tea.

6

Hans suggested we go out for a stroll with Zoya and Talia because it was Saturday. At the last minute Talia excused herself, leaving us three. He said we needed another girl: it didn't make sense for the two of us to be with one. Zoya called one of her girlfriends to join us, but she declined too. Zoya said, '*Nichevo,* it's OK. The three of us can go.'

We walked to the nearby park through the blowing snow. Whole families were out ice skating. Children in heavy clothing built a snowman. Zoya covered her head with a small, embroidered wool *shapka* which revealed the edges of her golden hair. My Russian was not good enough to follow their enthusiastic conversation. I just listened to her musical voice. Sometimes Hans would translate something she said into English. She was speaking in simple poetic childish words about scenes from nature and about her childhood. Suddenly her eyes welled up, and I discovered that she was speaking about the death of Khrushchev, or KhrushiOV, as they pronounce it.

I said I had been to his burial. I had heard the news in the morning from a journalist friend and had gone with him to the Novodevichy Cemetery. When we tried to enter, the guard stopped us. In front of us was an old woman, modestly dressed, with a wrinkled face and tear-stained eyes, a white shawl covering her head, and cork-soled shoes. She pleaded with the guard to let her in, repeating, '*Tovarish, tovarish.*' Finally, they let all of us enter. We passed the graves of leaders, scholars and artists, among them Chekhov, Gogol, Mayakovsky and the wives of Stalin and Kosygin. We reached the row reserved for this year's dead. We were surrounded by a few dozen people; my friend said that most of them were from the security services or foreign press. I was able to see the body in the grave. A tiny body with a pale face, quite unlike the familiar aura of vitality and power. When the words ended, everyone around him drifted away, each of us throwing a handful of dirt and pebbles into the grave.

Zoya wiped her eyes with the back of her gloved hand. 'They published the news of his death two days later, at the bottom of the front page of *Pravda*. In small print.' Hans put his arm around her, and they kissed deeply. He said it was like that everywhere: The loser in the struggle for power disappears from history. I didn't comment.

We decided to go downtown. We took a small bus to the metro station. Each of us paid 5 kopeks at the turnstile. We stood waiting for the train until it approached and jerked to a stop. Its door gaped open, letting out the Russian crowd smell: damp clothing, garlic, cabbage, wet leather. We pushed in between some cheerful young men wearing wool ski suits, on their way to Belorusskaya Station and the snowy forests. The driver shouted: '*Dveri zakrivayutsa*—the doors are closing!' We reached the station for Red Square. The giant chandeliers. The escalator. A group of Armenians selling tangerines. Women wrapped in shawls selling bouquets of flowers. Elderly *babushkas* bent under the baskets of goods they were carrying. And, finally, the street, and the snow, now falling more thickly and beginning to accumulate on the pavement. People walking carefully on the partly sand-strewn pavements. The thick fur-lined overcoats, the hats made of deerskin or genuine karakul and the tightly wrapped scarves. Invisible faces, only slits for the nose and eyes. Snowploughs everywhere and, beside them, the trucks spreading sand. Teams of women with shovels and wooden brooms cleaning the side streets. Others clearing snow from parked cars and leaving little cardboard squares under the windshield wipers signifying a 5-rouble fine for the owner. Some carrying torches to melt the ice from between the rails of the tram. A long queue of people waiting outside Lenin's tomb for a glimpse of his embalmed body.

We crossed the square to the Tomb of the Unknown Soldier and stood by the fence. I read the inscription addressing him: 'Your name is unknown, your deed immortal.' The inscription mentioned that the soldier had died on the airport road at the point where the Red Army had stopped the German advance towards Moscow. There were two soldiers guarding the tomb from small glass booths. When the time came for the changing of the guard, the two replacements goose-stepped out. A small crowd gathered. One of the old women cried.

Zoya said, in her poetic way, that at night the Kremlin's towers and the cathedrals' onion-shaped domes were lit up like something out of a fairy tale.

We walked around a little and passed by the GUM, the giant department store that sold everything. In the snow stood a man selling ice cream—or what they call *morozhenoye*—in his white uniform and snow boots. It stopped snowing; the sky turned grey. The mucus froze in my nose. Some cars went by: Volgas and Moskviches, sometimes passed by one or two ZiLs or Chaikas, the vehicles of the ruling class. We turned right at the TSUM store and stood looking at the tall columns of the Bolshoi Theatre and the four big bronze horses on the pediment above. We heard the Kremlin clock firmly strike noon. Leaving St Basil's Cathedral behind us, we went towards Sverdlov Square on the far side of Hotel Moskva. In front of it was a tourist bus with a few passengers gathered around. A nearby kiosk sold posters, newspapers and gifts. I started hopping up and down to fight the cold; my right hand was numb.

Zoya proposed that we have lunch in a *stolovaya*, a kind of popular cafeteria known for its low prices. For any one of your three meals, you wouldn't pay more than 3 roubles, or about 150 Egyptian piasters. We ate a lunch of salad, bread and fish soup, followed by rice or fried potatoes with beef or chicken or fish and fruit compote. All the time Brezhnev kept an eye on us from the wall above.

Hans was worried about the quality of the place: How clean was it? But Zoya said the women who cooked there always wore sterile clothes and covered their hair with white bonnets, and that the health inspector came every two months. She laughed, 'The health of the Soviet citizen is sacred. His sanity—that's another story.'

7

Jalaleddinov returned with his girlfriend Natasha. Blonde, Russian, eighteen. Modest and shy. I asked him how he got her in. He said, rubbing his thumb and fingers together in the universal gesture, 'I worked it out with the *dezhurnaya*.' He tacked up a blanket around his bed to block it from our view. At bedtime, he asked me to put on a Glinka record full of crashing drums and cymbals. Then he and his girl retired behind the curtain. Early in the morning, the girl snuck upstairs to the fifth floor, reserved for women, to wash her face in their bathroom.

I went out into the hall to do my morning calisthenics, then made some tea and offered her a cup. I sat down at the table in front of the Arabic typewriter.

The girl stayed in the room all day, not going out for fear of being discovered. In the evening, Jalaleddinov asked, 'Aren't you going to work at your typewriter?' 'No.' He then asked me to put on the Glinka again, and retired with his girlfriend behind the curtain.

8

I didn't go to the Institute the next day but stayed working at my typewriter. I exchanged some brief words with Natasha. I gathered that Jalal was from a family that had some status in his village and owned a lot of livestock. I said, 'You've got a difficult situation, stuck in a room with three men.' She laughed shyly, 'But we manage.'

'How?'

'When we ask you to put on the record player . . .'

She wanted to know if I was married. I said no.

The door banged open suddenly without a knock and Jalaleddinov burst in, his face flushed. He looked around, then pulled her behind the curtain. A sharp discussion ensued. I thought I heard her tell him that nothing had happened between us, we had only chatted briefly. After an hour they packed up and left the room.

I went out in the hall and passed by the room of Khalifa the Senegalese; he had the entire room to himself, thanks to the influence of his family or his tribe. The door was open and near it stood a mid-sized refrigerator. There was a Finnish girl stretched out on the bed, unbothered that her legs were open and showed everything all the way up to her underwear; she stared at the door, waiting. I caught a glimpse of Khalifa down the hall with some guys.

I knocked on the door of the Syrians' room. Hans opened it, and inside there was Zoya. She was sitting silent and worried on his bed. I learnt why when Hans announced his plan to travel that weekend to Yerevan, the capital of Armenia, with an Armenian student. Trying to lighten the mood, he told a Russian joke. 'So a listener asks Radio Yerevan: Is it possible for a man to become pregnant? Radio Yerevan responds: This has never been confirmed. However, experiments are currently underway in all corners of Armenia.'

Talia walked in, and Zoya accepted her kiss on the mouth without hesitation. I felt disgust, the same feeling that engulfs me when I see Arabs kissing each other on the lips. We told her the Armenian Radio joke. She said, 'I have a new one. One day in the metro, the passengers are surprised to see a man hit his forehead with his hand, hard, and shout, "How could this happen, you idiot, you ass, you son of a whore?" So the train inspector hurries over, "What's this you're saying? This is offensive to your fellow passengers and a violation of the law. You will be punished." The guy answers, "Just listen to my story . . . " Then the passengers are stunned to see the inspector hitting his forehead and shouting, "You idiot! You ass! You son of a whore!" The passengers can't stand it any more—they turn both of them in to the police. The officer asks what happened, so the passenger explains, "I'll tell you, comrade. I, as you can see, am white, with pink skin and yellow hair, and my wife is white and blonde also, and we just had a son who is a black Negro." So then the officer hits his forehead too and says, "How could this happen, you idiot, you ass, you son of a whore?"'

Hamid arrived soon after. He was chubby, about my height, with soft hair and a light moustache. He told me in Arabic that the Jordanian courts had just handed down death sentences to thirty-six Palestinian freedom fighters, and that Golda Meir, the prime minister of Israel, had praised what she had called 'King Hussein's courage and valour'.

9

Hans said he was going up to Zoya's room for tea. He invited me to come along. I remembered my plan to take a nap to be awake for that evening's party. I also felt that it would be pointless for me to be there with them. The conversation would be in Russian and boring. I declined.

I stretched out on the bed in my clothes. I felt like masturbating but held back, maybe from a kind of laziness. Or to avoid the pain it always brought on. I started drifting off to sleep, felt cold and got under the covers. Woke up to a knock on the door. I opened it and saw Zoya in front of me. She needed to borrow a knife. I looked for one, with my specs still off. I knelt down in front of the wardrobe to search in the bottom drawer. Out of the corner of my eye I noticed that she was wearing a short dress and that her legs were bare—no tights. I gave her the knife. She said she was making soup and invited me to come have some. She left, and I went back to bed. I felt weak. I wished someone would come and tell me the party had been cancelled. Or that I could sleep through until tomorrow. Or for Madeleine to suddenly show up. But then I imagined that I would have to see her out and walk her home afterwards, and then she would want to set a date to see me again—that made me drop the whole idea completely.

I tried to recall Zoya's features and the tone of her voice when I had opened the door. She was smiling. What would she have done if I had reached out and touched her bare leg when I was kneeling at the drawer?

I got out of bed. Deciding not to continue working at the typewriter on my report for my academic supervisor, I brushed my teeth, washed my face and made tea. Mario came in and went out again. The Kirghiz didn't show up. I thumbed through a book about Alexander the Great. Then I went out to the store. There was no vodka; they didn't sell it after 7 p.m. I bought a bottle of champagne for 4.76 roubles and a loaf of bread. When I got back to my room, Farid and Hamid were waiting.

Then Hind stopped by; I took the bottle and we all went down to the third floor. She was Iraqi, unusually light-skinned. Her Russian boyfriend Kolya joined us. We went outside in a sad procession. We got on the bus, putting our fares in the special box. I pulled out the ticket tape and cut one. Kolya walked past the box without paying and told me he usually didn't pay—life ought to be affordable for students. I stood by the door; an overweight Russian man told me to step in a little. Doing so let me get further away from Hind and her boyfriend. I stood in front of a seated Russian woman in her fifties with gold teeth and dyed hair. She was reading a book of poetry. Next to her, an African student carrying a James Brown record. The Russian man spoke to me again, asking me to move further towards the back of the bus. I did. I watched him focus on a book while holding a bag with several boxes of soap powder.

We transferred to the metro and I sat next to Hind. I asked her how old she was. She said, 'Twenty-three.' We started talking about Egypt. Biting her nails somewhat shyly, she asked me about the last time I been there. I told her my impression had been negative. She said she had passed through Alexandria on the ship and they had refused to let her disembark because they had suspected her of being Palestinian, but even so she had noticed how filthy the city was. I said it used to be clean in the past, when there had been foreigners. Now that it was ours we had messed it up.

We got off the train at Kutuzovskaya Station, the neighbourhood where the foreigners and diplomats lived. We walked between the sheets of glass and aluminium that decorated the station. We crossed the road and took another bus, then got off next to a church whose bells were ringing. We passed by new blocks of flats ten- or fifteen-storeys tall. An officer stopped us and asked where we were going. Hind told him her name. He asked her nationality and then pointed to Kolya, who kept quiet. I told him he had no right to question us. 'On the contrary . . . ' he replied. Then he hesitated and backed off. We walked up to one of the buildings. The glass door was locked; you could only open it if you had a key or knew your host's telephone number and punched in its last four numbers on a board. Farid did, and the door opened automatically. We went took the lift to the fourth floor. We were met by a gleaming parquet floor; on it stood Walid, welcoming us. He was about forty, plump, with thinning hair. We took off our shoes and coats. We entered a narrow room and saw a balcony door and a desk crammed with books and papers and a telephone, next to a crowded bookcase. On the other side, a table full of Syrian appetizers: hummus, tahina, garlic dip, stuffed baby eggplants and cabbage leaves and so on.

His wife Lamia was dark-skinned, heavy, in her thirties, with narrow eyes in a pale, sad face. She told me it was her husband who had prepared the *mezze* while she was taking care of their daughter, who had just turned seven months old. She asked me why I hadn't brought Madeleine. She had met her at the medical clinic and thought she was great. We sat around the table, and Kolya opened the champagne. We drank to the health of the baby, then Walid poured us vodka. He commented on the business with the police officer, saying he had the right to stop any Russian from entering the building—it was reserved for diplomats and foreign journalists, who needed to be kept away from contact with Russians. Then the talk turned to varieties of cheese, and Kolya said he adored Roquefort; he had once brought some to his mother in his village in Belorussia but she had almost thrown it away because of the smell. Walid pointed to the cheese on the table and said it was a good kind, called Sovetsky, that sold for 3.40 roubles a kilo and that it was no worse than more expensive kinds. Farid said he preferred Rossiyskiy. Kolya's stiff features lit up, and he joked, 'So you prefer Russia to the Soviet Union?'

Lamia brought in a plate of bologna. We asked about her. She said she was teaching in the school for Arab diplomats' kids and returned at 5 p.m., exhausted, to start the housework. Unkindly, I asked, 'Doesn't Walid help you?'

'No, he's always busy with his endless meetings— with Suheil Idris, Mustafa al-Hallaj, and before them Emile Touma and Mahmoud Darwish and Lotfi al-Kholi . . . And yesterday he stayed up late with Emile Habibi . . . There was a World Theatre Congress. And now he's getting ready for some film festival next month.'

Walid calmly replied that his meetings were useful, and that he was preparing a number of studies that would benefit everyone.

Wanting to change the subject, I asked him about the film by the Georgian director Iosseliani, *Once Upon a Time There Was a Singing Blackbird*. He said it had nice visuals but some conceptual weaknesses. He knew the director personally. Hamid said that Iosseliani's second film, attacking Stalin, had been banned since its release in 1963; strangely it was being screened in a few theatres now. Walid had informed the director when he met him a few days ago, so they had gone to see it with a group of friends. They had found that some parts were cut. Had any of us seen Pasolini's film *Oedipus Rex*? He carried on, without waiting for an answer, that it wasn't great—Pasolini had regressed since his first phase and started getting into religious rituals and stuff. Farid disagreed, but Walid ignored him, saying instead that the Polish director Wajda's play about Vietnam was now playing at the Taganka, and that he—Wajda—had staged *Hamlet* in a new style, 'casting a bright light on death on the curtain-less stage instead of concealing it in darkness like other directors.' Walid then dipped a stuffed cabbage leaf in oil and vinegar and shoved it in his mouth.

The telephone rang. I wished someone new would come. A couple, or a pair of girls. The phone call ended with an appointment to meet the following day. It rang again. This time I gathered that someone was coming over with his wife and a case of Stella.

'How did he get Egyptian beer here?' I asked Walid.

'It's available in lots of places. The USSR accepts anything Egypt can send to pay its debts.'

I sat down to wait, watching the door and listening for the lift. Finally the man and his wife arrived: Two fat white pigs, the sow in a trouser suit. The man took Walid aside and handed him a wad of dollars. Walid gave him roubles in exchange. He turned to us holding the dollars, 'If any of you need to exchange roubles, I'm at your service.' The conversation turned again to the police officer's attitude. Walid defended the authorities' right to keep Russians from contact with foreigners. He brought up a number of the Syrian students at the Institute as an example and said they were dumb, 'like bulls in a china shop.'

Hamid commented on the poor quality of some Soviet factory products, comparing them unfavourably with Western goods. I felt he was addressing Walid. I added that it was because market competition was prohibited, even though it improved quality. He said, 'So people have to buy the product because they can't find anything better.' 'Don't get me wrong, capitalist competition is no alternative,' I clarified. Walid welcomed my comment. He brought us a bottle of Stella and a dried fish, which he handed to Kolya, who cleaned it and made a big fuss over it. He told us his father had once made one such fish last a whole month because it was only available in the Berezka hard-currency stores. I enjoyed a little piece of it with the beer.

Walid monopolized the conversation again. His wife excused herself and went to bed. Eventually we got up to leave. Walid gave Hind a hug and asked her for a kiss on the cheek. Then he pulled her boyfriend aside and they talked quietly. Then he insisted we should drink more beer. He asked the most recent guest to stay behind; they had something important to discuss. We left the flat. We passed the police officer in his kiosk, making a point of speaking loudly in Arabic. Kolya complained of heartburn. Hind put her arm around him tenderly until we got on the bus. I stood next to Hamid and whispered, 'Isn't Walid afraid, openly exchanging hard currency like that?'

He laughed. 'The KGB oversees the currency trade. The state needs dollars.'

10

Jalaleddinov came back alone. He said he had rented a room in a nearby flat. Natasha would live with him there. But he would keep his bed in our room—we were not to say anything to anyone. Living outside the dormitory was forbidden.

11

I didn't sleep well. All night long there was a terrible noise from the room of the girls above me. And dance music blasted from Khalifa's room until 4 a.m. I was aroused by thinking of Zoya, and my penis began to hurt. I pictured us going out alone together, her slender body suddenly in my arms, my eyes gazing into hers.

I walked to the bathroom, bringing my empty milk bottle to the sink to fill with water so I could wash myself instead of using the rough toilet paper. Khalifa the Senegalese was standing in front of the last sink in the corner. He wanted to wash himself too. He took off his underpants and stuck his large penis right under the faucet to wash it, giving me a smug look.

I decided to work at the typewriter. I lifted it up to carry it to the table, but it fell on the floor; the plastic frame smashed. I put it aside angrily. Hamid came and tried to cheer me up. We went out together to the nearby *pivnaya* and drank tasteless Russian beer. I told him about my battle with my ambitious colleague Hilmi Abdullah, a member of the Arab Socialist Union and my rival for the love of our colleague Gamalat. He ended up getting her.* On our way back we ran into

Bashar. He had bought some good meat from the Berezka and invited us for dinner. He was Syrian, medium height, and had grown his smooth hair down to his shoulders Western-style.

We put the tray of meat in the oven of the first-floor kitchen and sat there while it broiled so no one would steal it. Then we ate in the Syrians' room, washing it down with what was left of a bottle of wine. Farid joined us. He said Israel had conducted eight hours of bombing raids on Syria and that Zoya had brought Hamid a book an hour ago and then vanished. Hans went upstairs to invite her down but didn't find her. We drank vodka with some new arrivals: Abbas the Iraqi, just back from a visit home to Iraq; a Lebanese guy named Jean; and Helene, Bashar's Greek girlfriend. Her extremely short skirt showed her spectacular legs; their beauty filled me with sadness. She sat quietly while we spoke in Arabic. Hamid asked Abbas about an Iraqi student who had graduated from the Institute and returned to Iraq.

'*Maku*,' Abbas said.

'And what about Abdel Gabbar?'

'*Maku*.'

I asked him what that meant; he moved a silent index finger across his throat. Then he told how the Ba'athists had captured a union leader, raped his wife, stolen his money, then forced him to have sex with a boy and taken photos to blackmail him; they threatened to expose him in front of the workers, so he gave in to their demands. Then he said Saddam Hussein had debuted in politics while in high school, leading one of the armed terrorist groups persecuting Communists after the overthrow of Abdel Karim Qasim.

'What about the anti-Ba'ath conspiracy, or what the Soviet newspapers described as an imperialist plot to bring down the nationalist regime?' I asked.

'Fabrication. A Ba'athist excuse to round up the Nasserists, with the Soviet Union's support.'

Farid asked him how it was that Aziz al-Haj, the leader of the militant Communist Party Central Command, had confessed and gone to work for the regime. He said it was simple. 'The Ba'ath authorities executed several comrades in front of him one after another, first mutilating them, especially their genitals.' He then described how they had tried to assassinate Kurdish leader Mustafa al-Barzani.

12

I invited Zoya and Hans to a concert at the Bolshoi, a Mozart quartet. Hans said no, he had to work on his thesis. Zoya went upstairs to wash her hair, and I brushed my teeth. We left the *obshchezhitie* together, her hands in her coat pockets. We walked to the conservatory in silence. The old lady at the cloakroom counter proudly refused my tip; she informed me that she still had a poster from the time of the Revolution that read, 'Tips not accepted here.' She added, 'If some people are forced to serve others to earn a living, that's no reason to insult them with tips.'

The theatre was crowded and we couldn't find two seats together. Zoya found a seat in the second row, and I sat in the last row next to a Kazakh girl. I got distracted, couldn't focus and felt bored. At intermission, I hurried towards the buffet. A dark pretty face caught my eye. I recognized her: the Egyptian girl who worked as a servant for one of the employees at the Egyptian embassy. She was with a Russian young man whose fastidious attire betrayed his humble origins. She recognized me and looked uncomfortable. I met Zoya and we approached the buffet. We had a beer; I invited her to have some food but she declined. The second half of the concert was livelier. When we met afterwards, she said she was *svobodnaya zhenshina*, a free woman, because her secondment period from 7 p.m. to 10 p.m. was over—she was no longer on loan. She busied herself looking at the posters for upcoming concerts. I said Hans wanted to go hear the Bach. She said bitterly that he was going home to the GDR.

I walked with her to the metro station, finding it difficult to keep the conversation going. She said something I didn't catch about the movement of the train pushing her towards me. She repeated again that she was a free woman. 'Watch out!' I said. She carried on about how she had passed that month's exams with flying colours because the instructor thought she was cute, and here she had always been convinced she was ugly—in school they had nicknamed her Skeleton. I nearly hugged her.

At the *obshchezhitie* entrance she promised to stop by my room for some tea. In the hall I ran into Hans wandering around drunk; he said he was hungry. He asked me what we had been up to; I said it was a boring evening. I made him come up to the fifth floor with me to look for Zoya. We didn't find her. When we came down again, we were surprised to find her in his room. I noticed she had freshened her lipstick. He asked, 'Where have you been? I was looking for you.' But she pointed to me, and said, 'No. He was the one looking for me.' He kissed her on the mouth, then looked at her with contempt and said a word to her in German that meant she was a slut. She repeated the word without understanding. I opened a bottle of beer and expressed my objection to his word choice by not offering him any. He walked around us and said he hoped nothing would happen between us, and she hurried to reply, 'It won't.' He said he wanted to take her to Bashar's room, which was empty. But he didn't have the key. I said, 'Go to my room, there's no one there.'

13

On Saturday afternoon I went with Farid, Bashar and Helene to visit Farid's Russian girlfriend, who lived an hour and a half away by train. We walked down a short narrow residential street: four-storey red-brick block of flats emitting boisterous music. The birch trees looked naked and cold without their leaves. The stairwell reeked of cabbage. We entered a one-bedroom flat floored in grey linoleum. Inside: a table, an armchair and a bed covered with a wool blanket. On the table: a pair of spectacles, some medicine bottles and a copy of *Pravda*. On the wall: pictures of Lenin, medals of socialist labour and a certificate of recognition for forty years of Communist Party membership. We were met by Farid's girlfriend Irma and her mother. The former was taller than Farid, in her early twenties, with a childlike face. The latter had the typical Russian build and a face suggesting a strong personality. 'She's a good Communist,' Farid told me in Arabic. 'She lost her husband 15 years ago. She works as a nurse and once had to change jobs because she couldn't keep quiet about the doctor's chronic stealing.'

The flat was extremely hot, which I pointed out. The mother said, 'In the past, people used to freeze to death, but not any more.' Irma snapped, 'Now they die for other reasons.'

Helene took off her overcoat and revealed her amazing legs. The mother disappeared into the kitchen. Irma turned on the TV, and we watched a film denouncing alcoholism. She told us, laughing, about an old man who had been taken to the police station for excessive drunkenness. When they had asked why he had turned to the bottle, he'd said it was the only thing that made him feel human for a moment.

We opened bottles of champagne and vodka and exchanged toasts. Irma showed us her photo album and a volume of poetry by Isaac Babel. Tortured by the Soviet secret police in Lubyanka Prison in 1939, he had accused his friends, then recanted his confession, and been executed on Stalin's orders the following year on a bogus charge of espionage. Then in 1954, after Stalin's death, they had rehabilitated him. The mother grimaced at this line of conversation; Irma responded by sarcastically chanting, 'Long live the great Stalin, father and teacher of the Soviet peoples, the great inspiration for the triumph of Communism, leader of all progressive mankind!' The mother remarked, 'In Stalin's time the place used to be clean. These days anywhere you look all you find is drinking, depravity and drugs, men beating their wives half to death, communal flats full of bickering.' Evidently it was an ongoing argument between the two of them.

To change the subject, Farid offered that we would soon see America defeated in Vietnam. We spent the rest of the evening drinking vodka, playing cards and dancing. Farid did an imitation of me doing my calisthenics and we all laughed. At 3 a.m., drunk, I danced with Irma and got an erection. Bashar danced with his girlfriend. He moved confidently, his long hair flowing around his head.

We all slept on the living-room floor while the women took the bedroom. In the morning I had a terrible headache. The mother gave me an aspirin and Vitamin C and advised me to drink some beer for the hangover. We went for a walk. Beautiful weather; the snow had stopped. The balconies were crowded with various junk: bed and bicycle frames, old car parts, dead plants. Some were draped with banners: 'Self-criticism Is the Cornerstone of Our Party'; 'From Fire Emerges Steel.' We discussed the problem of Muslims and Christians in Egypt. Then we went back to the house and resumed drinking and playing cards. I was the most cheerful of them. Meanwhile the mother sat silently next to me, then got up and brought us a plate of mushrooms with sour cream and garlic.

We left late Sunday afternoon. Farid stayed behind without enthusiasm. On the train I read a little of Arthur Koestler's novel, *Darkness at Noon*, which criticizes the Soviets. Hans had given it to me. Most of the passengers looked exhausted after Saturday's excesses. There was a sleeping husband whose wife was reading, until he woke up and snarled at her to move her leg which was on top of his. We got off the train and boarded the metro along with an old woman carrying a guitar. I noticed a man sleeping on a seat, alone, with his hand over his mouth. There was also an officer whom, by his accent, we identified as a Syrian. He was with a pretty girl who wore a wedding ring. When he greeted us, she said, 'More countrymen of yours,' and stared at us. She was wearing a lemon-yellow wig-shaped bonnet. He must have brought it for her from Syria, or Helsinki, or the Berezka, I thought, and he must have been on a training mission or part of a visiting delegation. At one stop when the driver announced over the intercom that the doors would be opening, the officer said something to her and laughed. When we got off the metro, they exited before us and were joined by another Syrian officer, this one with a woman who looked like a prostitute. They stood apart as we stood waiting for the bus, the two officers showing the girls various military drill movements and laughing.

14

Hans opened the door of my room and said, 'Here he is.' Zoya was beside him, wearing a knee-length blue tunic with Chinese embroidery over a pair of green trousers. '*Zdrastvuy*,' she greeted me. I answered her, but my voice came out strange. Hans stared at me. She said she had not slept here the night before. I ignored this. She asked, 'Why do you seem so down?' I blamed low blood pressure. She said there was a medicine for that. Then she complained to Hans, 'Why don't you ever say beautiful things to me?' Then she told a new joke: 'A few decades in the future, a foreign journalist asks a Soviet citizen about Brezhnev and Kosygin. He responds, "Oh, they were two politicians who lived in the age of the writer Solzhenitsyn."' I forced a laugh. They left.

At 4.30 the weather became oppressive and sad. I put on my overcoat and picked up the typewriter with the pieces of its case. I walked to the metro, then rode to Marx Prospect. I went into a typewriter repair shop. I handed over the typewriter to a sullen worker, who told me to come back for it in a month. I headed for the restaurant behind the Bolshoi Theatre. I stood outside the restaurant in the cold for an hour. The guard was moving haughtily, letting people into the restaurant in stages: first into the space between the two sets of glass doors, where the warm air felt good, and then inside the restaurant. I took off my coat and ordered a half chicken *tabaka*.

Afterwards I headed to the cinema. I watched *Once Upon a Time There Was a Singing Blackbird*. The protagonist played tympani in an orchestra and always arrived just in time to deliver the two drumbeats at the end, which was his only responsibility. I felt like crying when the film ended with him dying in a car accident because he had turned to stare at a woman passing by.

I bought *morozhenoye*, ice cream, and knocked on Hans' door. He answered wearing an open bathrobe that bulged below the waist. I thought he might have an erection. He approached and bent down to kiss my neck; I backed away. He went back in and got dressed behind the wardrobe that stood the width of the room. He made coffee. I decided that if I saw Zoya, I would ignore her. A few minutes later she knocked on the door and came in covering her mouth with her hand, saying playfully, 'I have a cold.' I found myself smiling and saying to her, 'I bought *morozhenoye*.' She clapped her hands rapturously and sat down in the armchair. I put my hand on her hair and pulled her head to my chest. We had *café glacé*, coffee with *morozhenoye*. She left her chair and sat on Hans' lap. He started explaining to her the meaning of the word *frigid*.

'Like her,' I said.

'How would you know?' he asked. 'On the contrary!'

'How would *you* know?'

'Really, how would you know?' Zoya joined in.

'Her husband told me,' Hans replied.

We laughed. I went back to my room and left them together.

15

In the morning Hans knocked on my door and asked if I had seen the girl. I said no. He had seen her with a pack of Egyptian cigarettes and kicked her out the night before, so he thought maybe she had come crying to me.

'That's me, the shoulder to cry on.'

He laughed.

I went to the Institute to pick up my passport and to find out about the trip to Leningrad. Farid said the Americans had signed a ceasefire agreement in Vietnam. I wondered how the world would look now since we were so used to hearing war news every day? He said Israel had annexed Syria's Golan Heights. I stole a glance at the second floor and saw tables, sandwiches, beer, apples, tomatoes and strangers. Farid said it was a conference of the Communist Party members in the neighbourhood. They were dressed in their Sunday best and wearing lapel pins with Lenin's photo. One of the Institute's professors passed near me. He was carrying an open briefcase; inside I glimpsed a large, unwrapped piece of meat and nothing else.

Back at the *obshchezhitie* I stopped by the Syrians' room. Zoya was sitting on Hans' bed in her blue miniskirt. She asked me, 'Are you going to the Communist Party conference? They're selling meat, apples and tomatoes.'

I laughed.

'Why are you laughing?'

'You're full of questions.'

She got upset and buried herself in a newspaper. Hans borrowed two glasses from me, saying Vladimir had brought a bottle of vodka. He invited me to join them, but I declined.

I decided to do my laundry. After an hour Hans appeared, looking miserable. He said he needed some sugar to make coffee. He also said he had just spent an hour sitting in silence while Zoya had a pretentious bourgeois conversation with Vladimir.

16

I headed to the Institute with Farid and Hamid. Hamid said he remembered the first time he came to Moscow. He kept repeating that he would grab the world by the horns. Now he felt like his huge reservoir of energy was all used up. I went to meet with my academic supervisor. He was around fifty, wearing trousers that clashed with his jacket. He listened to me absentmindedly and signed my proposal. I went to the cashier for my monthly stipend, double what the Soviet students got.

I went to Health Clinic #6 downtown, the one we were assigned to. I undressed and described my condition to him, drawing a penis and testicles on a piece of paper, before lying down on the doctor's examination bench. He told me to hold my penis in my hand. Then he put on a white glove and stuck his finger into my anus, moving it until I felt a burning sensation. He said I had an inflamed prostate because of the cold. He prescribed some ointment, enemas and a massage of the gland he said he would do himself. I walked to the Arbatskaya Station, then switched trains at Kievskaya.

17

Mario returned excited from a trip with the Brazilian students to a village a thousand kilometres away. He said the villagers eat well; meat and tomatoes are widely available, and they never tire of reminiscing about the Second World War.

I decided to go out, perhaps to the embassy. The sky was grey and it was pouring, so I decided to skip it. After an hour I went out and took the bus, then the metro, to Taganka Station. I headed for the Foreign Literature Library. I asked for the novel *The Comedians* by Graham Greene. Next to me were a dried-up old woman and an ugly young woman. Their attention was on the art books. At five o'clock I felt sleepy and nodded off several times for a few minutes each. I smoked a cigarette in the smoking room, which was somewhat cold because of the smoke ventilator. A girl walked in for a smoke and I wished, stealing a glance at the edge of her leg from the corner of my eye, that I could talk to her.

I left the library and crossed the street to the cinema, which was showing an old American film by John Ford. The next show was sold out. I walked carefully on the ice to Taganka Square. The air smelt of car exhaust. I went into a cafe and stood for a few minutes. The blood came back to my face and ears, and my specs fogged up. I wiped them with my handkerchief. I told the cashier I wanted macaroni, *shchi* soup, a *kotleta* meat patty and coffee. I paid 50 kopeks and stood in line. I took two spoonfuls of the cabbage soup, ate the macaroni and meat without appetite and drank the coffee. There was an old woman in full make-up eating and reading while standing up at a table.

I put on my hat and gloves and headed for another cinema. There was a show starting in an hour: a Bulgarian spy film. I bought a ticket and lit a cigarette. The made-up old lady came and bought a ticket as well. I went and used the bathroom downstairs, then came back up and took a seat in a room where seats were lined up in front of a small stage. I saw people heading inside and followed them to the concession stand, where I got a bottle of beer and some *konfety*, candy. Then I returned to the auditorium. A group of musicians appeared, two of them women. They played a few pieces without enthusiasm, including the song 'Tell me' and a Schubert serenade sung by a woman in a sleeveless evening gown, followed by a pretty Uzbek dance song. One of the female musicians was sitting so that only the side of her face could be seen; I wished I could see more. She reminded me of Gamalat. I recalled that I was always disappointed every time I saw a face in profile and then saw the whole thing.

A bell rang, and I headed for the screening room. I sat next to a man who looked exhausted and depressed. The screening began with a short colour film about the splendour of life in the Far East and their metal mines, and another, Bulgarian, about a modern city being rebuilt after the war. Then Zhivkov, the Bulgarian Communist Party leader, appeared, cutting ribbons at factories and schools. Then, finally, began the spy film. It was a dumb story about a spy trying to collect intelligence about the civil defence programme. The film began with a speech by a big general about the role of civil defence in a nuclear war. A handsome but bad actor played the protagonist—a painter specialized in icon restoration who outwits the foreigners until he falls into the clutches of a foreign journalist-spy. The film ended suddenly; I could not understand why. The woman behind me said she didn't get it at all, and her companion objected, looking around in embarrassment, 'What do you mean? Everything was clear.' A young man next to them said, 'The next instalment will explain the rest.' Another one complained, '60 kopeks—that's three bottles of beer we could have bought.'

I hurried to the metro and rode to the bus stop. I stood waiting for a long time in the snow. In the bus I heard a lot about the unprecedented weather. One passenger read aloud from his newspaper: 'In the past five days, Moscow has received more than 30 million cubic metres of snow, piled more than 36 centimetres high in the streets.'

The *dezhurnaya* had a letter for me; it was from my friend Kamal. He warned me not even to think of returning to Egypt. They were arresting people. I stopped by to see Hans and invited him to my room. I turned on the electric heater. We made tea. I told him what Mario had said about the village. He laughed, 'It's a model village, specially assembled to leave a positive impression of the comforts of village life.' He left when he saw me preparing the enema. I knelt on the bed, lifting one leg until my knee touched my nose, and enjoyed the warm water flowing inside me. Then I set my alarm clock to eight. I sprayed my chest and armpits with the cologne Madeleine had given me. I wrapped myself up in the blanket, enjoying the smell of the perfume around me, and slept.

18

I worked at the repaired typewriter, accompanied by Tchaikovsky's 'Symphony No. 5'. Its sad melodies reminded me of what Hans had said about the Tchaikovsky statue downtown, how the effeminate gesture of its left hand alluded to the composer's homosexuality. I went to the kitchen to make a cup of tea. I knocked on the door of the Syrians' room and turned the knob. To my surprise, Hans was standing there with someone in his arms. The daylight from the window was in my face. At first I thought it was Vladimir, but then I saw it was Zoya leaning against his shoulder. She turned towards me and I gave her a hug. I told her Hans had been looking for her. 'I know that's not true,' she groused. She handed me a present—a pen—and announced she was going to shower and then go to Vladimir's room. He was painting her portrait. I returned to my room and began reading Solzhenitsyn's novel *Cancer Ward*. Farid knocked on the door. He had heard on the radio that Israel had shot down a Libyan civilian plane. I went out to buy milk, cognac and a copy of *Literaturnaya Gazeta*. I bought Indian tea, bread and Moroccan sardines. When I returned I met Hans in the hallway. He was on his way up to the fifth floor. Two hours later he came to my room with Vladimir and a bottle of homemade vodka. Vladimir was Ukrainian, in his twenties, overweight, sloppily dressed. Hans said he was returning to Germany the following day. Vladimir said he would never marry someone unless she was a virgin. Zoya came, wearing a blouse with long red stripes. Vladimir blushed and did not take his eyes off her. I told them what Solzhenitsyn had said about the children whose parents were purged by Stalin: they were made to write denunciations of their dead or deported fathers and mothers. And what Lenin had announced in 1917 about the need to give higher salaries to skilled labourers. Zoya said she had learnt a few expressions in German, among them *Ich liebe dich*, I love you. We were silent for a long moment. Zoya kept her eyes on Hans. He was trim and handsome, with hair falling over his forehead. Zoya asked me what was the matter with me. 'Nothing,' I said. She knew exactly what the matter was. How amazing for her to sit among three men, knowing they all loved her in different ways. Vladimir poured her one glass after another. Was he trying to get her drunk? He got up and put on 'The Last Waltz' which she liked because you could dance to it. Hamid joined us, then Talia, and they danced with her. I switched off the overhead light and turned on the desk lamp. Zoya sat on top of the wooden dresser, her expression suggesting that one of us should ask her for a dance. Hans was starting to look drunk. I put another bottle on the table—*pertsovaya* vodka. I glanced from Zoya to Hans to see if he was looking at me, then quickly at Vladimir to see if he was looking at her. Zoya bent down towards Hans and kissed him on the mouth. He got up and pulled her by the arm as she resisted playfully. She followed him as far as the door of the room. They whispered together. Then she came back and sat down again and finished her cigarette. From the corner of my eye I watched her pick up her sweater and calmly put it on. Then she stood up and said, '*Spokoynoy nochi,* good night.' She looked at me for a moment, then left the room, followed by Hans. We sat around for a little while longer; I looked out the window. Then everyone left and I started preparing my enema.

19

I cleaned my room. Hans arrived. He said Farid and Hamid had been out the night before, so Zoya had stayed with him; she was still there, in his room. She had received a letter from her husband saying he was ill, he had pneumonia, and she was going to visit him. He paced the room aimlessly, then said, 'I left her alone with Vladimir for three hours yesterday, then I took her to bed.' He was silent for a minute, and then added, 'You should have seen her saying goodbye to him. Like their cheeks were stuck together.' He went to the bathroom while I walked to his room ahead of him. I found her curled up in a ball on the floor under the desk. She was wearing the chic blue blouse that looked like a military uniform. She asked, 'How did you find me?'

'I saw you with my heart.'

'Let's see if Hans will know where I am.'

'He has a lot on his mind.'

Hans came and asked, 'Where is she?' Then he saw her. She pointed to a picture of herself that she had drawn and hung on the wall over his bed. On the top, she had written *Dobroye utro*, good morning, and on the bottom, *Spokoynoy nochi*. She said she would draw one for me, too. I said, 'If I looked at that before bedtime, it wouldn't be a peaceful sleep.' Her sentimentality and childlike manner repulsed me. She had brought a jar of preserves and went to look for some bread and butter. It was a brand-new jar, elegant, from Romania. I thought she might have got it as a present from Vladimir.

'Do you think she gave him anything?' Hans asked.

'I don't think so.'

He pointed out Vladimir's effeminate movements. Zoya returned with the bread and butter; we had breakfast. I asked her where she had got the preserves; she thought for a long time, then named a shop. Probably she was lying. She read us a short story she had written the day before. A fable about two suns and some flowers, and one of the suns had been taken over by a creeping coldness. She asked Hans if he would come with her to the metro station. He said he was tired and she could get there by herself. As I prepared to leave, she kissed me on the cheek and said she would stop by and visit me when she returned. She added, '*Ne skuchayte bez menia*, don't be lonely without me.'

I took my enema and felt very aroused. I locked the door and lay face down on top of a pillow. I pictured the thighs of Vera the Jewish girl in her miniskirt. I moved my body back and forth until I felt the shudder of pleasure. Then I read a little and found myself dozing. After a while I woke up. I thought of calling up Larissa and inviting her to dinner. I had met her with two of her girlfriends in a bookshop in Cairo. They were working at the Soviet embassy. She was tall and graceful, with a pretty face. The idea didn't excite me. Perhaps because I had once smelt her breath, or because she was so obviously trying to find a husband. I imagined how the conversation would go and when I would start feeling bored and wishing I could be rid of her.

20

The doctor inserted his finger in my anus and began the prostate massage. He was dark-skinned and seemed to be from one of the non-Russian minorities. He said, in an aggressive tone that surprised me, that he needed a new tyre for his car, a Volkswagen. So could I get him one?

'How?'

'From your country's embassy.'

I told him I didn't know anyone there. He finished the massage and snarled, 'So I'm sticking my finger up your ass and you don't bring me so much as a bottle of whisky?'

I ignored him.

21

We got together with Zoya in the Syrians' room after she returned from visiting her husband. Hamid, Farid, Vladimir and I. She told us how she had found the silly kitchen girl madly in love with him, following him around. And how the conscripts got drunk one night and opened the officers' storehouse and took three bottles of vodka and replaced them later, half filled with water. She recalled how she had met her husband when she was in the Pioneers and wearing a red neckerchief. She didn't love him at the beginning but married him to escape from her mother's control. Their first night was frustrating. She suddenly asked, 'Any news from Hans? When's he coming back?' Then, looking at me, she said, 'I know my relationship with him will end one way or another.' She said she disliked shy, modest people.

Vladimir joined the conversation. *Sovetskaya Kultura*, the Central Committee's new newspaper, had criticized the film and theatre star Vladimir Vysotsky who had become very popular among the youth for his husky voice and his dissident songs satirizing the Soviet regime. He quoted one of Vysotsky's ballads:

My motherland, my blood pours out for you.
And yet my heart is hot with indignation:
My blood's spilt for Serezhka Fomin, too
While he sits there like someone on vacation.

I bet he's at the movie house right now,
And us—we're in the newsreel that they're
        showing.
I'd love to get Serezhka here somehow,
To taste just how the German front is going.

But finally the war is at an end
We heaved it off our shoulders like a burden.
I meet Fomin one time, and on his chest
A medal: 'Hero of the Soviet Union.'*

Zoya said some of his songs dealt with the labour
camps in Siberia, including this one :

They locked us up for a misunderstanding, see,

Him for embezzlement and me for Ksenia,

[…]

The Cheka threw us in

With common criminals:

Convict Vasilev and Petrov the Con.**

22

An Egyptian journalist gave me his whole collection of Egyptian newspapers because his time in the Moscow bureau was up. I brought it in two taxis to the Institute. It took several trips to carry them all to my room. The *komendantsha* saw me and pursed her lips but said nothing. I put the newspapers in a corner of the room, where they made a tall pile. I thought in dismay of the task awaiting me. I found the newspapers of the six days of June 1967 and began to read. I picked up a pair of scissors and clipped some of the contents. I dripped a few drops of glue onto a clean piece of paper, stuck on the clippings and wrote the date. Then I picked up another newspaper.

23

I had put aside Thornton Wilder's novel about Julius Caesar. I picked it up again and reread a passage that had caught my attention:

> It is by poets that all men are told that we press forward to a Golden Age and they endure the ills they know in the hope that a happier world will arrive to rejoice their descendants. Now it is very certain that there will be no Golden Age and that no government can ever be created which will give to every man that which makes him happy, for discord is at the heart of the world and is present in each of its parts. It is very certain that every man hates those who have been placed over him; that men will as easily relinquish the property they have as lions will permit their food to be torn away from between their teeth.

And another passage:

> [W]e rulers must be not only wise but supernatural, for in their eyes human wisdom is helpless before magic. We must be at once the father they knew in their infancy who guarded them against evil men and the priest who guarded them against evil spirits.*

24

Mario said he had heard on Voice of America that eight Palestinian guerrillas had attacked the Saudi embassy in Khartoum and executed three foreign diplomats. He said he would be out that night, so I called Madeleine. She came in the afternoon. She needed to pee, and I suggested she go up to the girls' floor. She refused. Instead she went to a corner of the room and used the empty milk bottle. I lay down on the bed and began to read peacefully. I thought that marriage must be pretty relaxing from that point of view. She came up and stretched out beside me. I held her, but she took a long time to respond; I lost interest and fell asleep. We slept until morning.

Madeleine didn't leave the room till I pressed her to go up to the bathroom on the fifth floor. I went out to buy some groceries and a bottle of wine. While I was making lunch, Adnan came by the kitchen. Mid-twenties, handsome face and straight hair. I invited him to eat with us; he didn't object. He sat down and began to talk about himself and his drawings. He made fun of the bottle of wine, saying that this kind was weak and offering to go out and buy something stronger. He did so and returned with a stack of records, including one of contemporary Egyptian music. He played the one called, 'The Bathtub Told Me, Get Up and Wash'. He claimed that it was an Egyptian folk song but I snapped, 'That's not folklore or anything, that's just crap.' He took it off the player and put on Muhammad Abdel Wahab's 'Ah mennak ya garehni'—Oh, You've Wounded Me. He followed that with a song by Farid al-Atrash and then one by Charles Aznavour. Was that his playlist when he invited a girl to *his* room? He wanted to put on one more, but I said, 'Enough! The girl has to leave soon and I want some time alone with her.' He ignored me and played the soundtrack of Raj Kapoor's *Sangam*. I stretched out on the bed. He gathered his records and got up to leave. But then, embarrassed, she asked him to stay a little longer. He left anyway after a short while. I yelled at her. Then we had sex and came together, forgetting to do anything about the pregnancy thing. Afterwards, she said, 'I wish you'd kiss me when we do it.' I got curious about the roots of her masochism. She said she had gone to Catholic schools; as a teenager she had masturbated after hearing torture stories about the holy martyrs. Her grades had been good, but she would always commit some small misdeeds so she would be punished and made to kneel for an hour. I asked her about the first time she had masturbated. She said, 'I was sitting in class distracted, and got scared that the teacher would punish me for it . . . the thought of it aroused me, and I started rubbing myself on the chair.'

She refused to go upstairs to the women's bathroom but peed in the milk bottle, putting a page of one of my newspapers under the bottle. I exploded with anger at her. Then I felt some dizziness and pain over my eye and then in my leg. We went to bed again. Both times I made no effort to hold back and wait for her. She didn't need me to.

25

The next day I received a postcard from her that said, in English: 'As I was leaving the *obshchezhitie* I met Adnan and he wanted to know why you hadn't walked me to the bus. I wanted to tell him to mind his own business, but I didn't, because I'm polite. That's right! Now I understand why he made you angry.'

Mario watched me working with the newspapers. He asked what I was doing. I told him I was following up on the important events of recent years. And that I had a vague idea of a huge project it would lead to. He looked impressed. I put on Muhammad Abdel Wahab's 'Al-Nil Nagashi' and sat down at the table to think. I had been reading a month's newspapers in a day, then resting the following day. At this rate, I would need several months.

At the end of the night I gathered all the newspaper scraps I had thrown on the floor and went out into the hall. I put them into the garbage can in the kitchen. Then I came back and lit a cigarette. I opened the transom window to let out the smoke.

26

I got up early. Some rays of sunshine were sneaking into the room. I took a knife and walked across the wood floor to the window. Then I cut the paper that was stuck between the panes to protect from draughts in the winter. I pulled up the handle and let in the cool, refreshing air. I watched a crane lift a load of red bricks for the workers to pile, row upon row, at the nearby building project. I took a rag, wet it and scrubbed the traces of adhesive from the windowpane. It was the cleaning lady's day off. In the past, the students had done the cleaning for themselves, but the Egyptians had protested and refused. I sat down at the table and picked up a newspaper. A little while later, I gathered the scraps of cut-up newspapers and carried them out of the room.

I went with Hamid to the Institute. There was a delicious nibbling chill in the air and a warm sun overhead. I took huge gulps of the fresh air. He told me about an anti-Zionist novel, *The Promised Land*, by a young Soviet writer. The protagonist, a young Romanian Jew, emigrates to Palestine to flee the Nazis. He has no religious or ideological motivations, he's just trying to save his skin. A Zionist tells him Herzl once said that if Hitler had not existed, we would have invented him ourselves—if Nazism hadn't existed, with its racial theory, the overwhelming majority of our brethren would never have found their way to the Promised Land. However, the immigrant uncovers some horrifying truths in that land and leaves, never to return.

The ice had begun to melt, and the municipal authorities had applied chemicals to help it along. Hamid said the temperature was up to 7 or 8 above 0. Which didn't mean that spring had arrived: it could be a false thaw. I noticed that the pedestrians' clothes were stained with water and mud from the dripping roofs and gutters. I saw workers in black jackets piling up the snow with iron shovels. The road filled with garbage and debris that had been buried under the snow. The benches were covered with plywood to prevent anyone from sitting on them. Hamid said that meant the rooftops were being cleared; many people had been killed by falling snow and ice. We ran into Farid. He said today was the seventeenth straight day of Israeli air attacks on the Syrian city of Harra. And that Sadat was building a prison for 13,000 people in the Oasis. He added that the communists in Syria and Iraq were collecting donations for their Egyptian comrades who had been expelled from the Arab Socialist Union.

27

The men gathered around the rose vendors. In the metro, every man carried a bouquet, and a group of young people gathered around a singer with a guitar. Some of the girls and women were dressed up and cheerful, others gloomy. It was 8 March, International Women's Day.

I went to Cafe Elite to meet Abdel Hakim. An Egyptian, around forty, stout and bald. Sweet and shy. He was from one of the first cohorts sent by Nasser to study in the USSR; he had settled down, married a Ukrainian woman and found a job in the Arabic division of the Russian broadcasting service.

The cafe was crowded and we barely found a table. I noticed two girls looking for a spot. They asked if they could join us. We agreed, of course. We introduced ourselves. They were in their early twenties. Natasha was blonde with a baby face, wearing a red blouse and black trousers; she was in her fourth year at the Institute of Nutrition. The other one was Lamara: thin, with curly hair parted Gypsy-style, wearing a sweater and a skirt. Her face looked very sensual; she didn't tell us her profession. She said Women's Day was the only day of the whole year when men did all the women's chores. Abdel Hakim said his wife was away on a trip and suggested we move to his flat. It was close to the cafe, in a modern building, well heated and consisting of a bedroom and a living room with two sofas facing each other. Lamara sat next to me on one sofa and Natasha sat next to Abdel Hakim on the other. He brought a bottle of whisky and some snacks. Natasha said she couldn't drink; she had a heart condition. Nonetheless she smoked greedily. She said she had got married in her first year at the Institute and divorced within a year; she was working at a toy store until she could receive a Moscow residence permit. She turned pale after a little while and stretched out on the couch, resting her head on Abdel Hakim's thigh; she said she got tired really fast and needed to rest every so often. Abdel Hakim held her hand. Lamara sipped her whisky. She said she had a child whom she had left with her mother in Tbilisi, the capital of Georgia. Natasha ruminated about not finding a reason to go on living. She showed me her palm and pointed to the short lifeline. Lamara told a Brezhnev joke, imitating his manner of speaking: 'In two years, Citizens, each of you will have a flat, and in five years a car, and in seven years ... a helicopter.' My mind wandered, studying her face with its sensual lips. I said Sadat had promised to give every citizen access to the electron. Lamara laughed and put her hand on my leg. I felt some kind of thread running between the two of us. We kissed, and I asked her to go shower; she did this without objection. I spread a blanket on the floor. I turned off the light and we lay down. Abdel Hakim stayed on the couch holding Natasha's hand. Lamara's jutting hipbones bothered me, and I found her too loose. I turned her over face down and came alone. During the night I felt her spreading the blanket over me. Next morning she seemed sad. I saw Abdel Hakim and Natasha sound asleep on the couch, fully dressed. He was still holding her hand.

28

I saw Lamara two days later; Natasha wasn't along. We went to Abdel Hakim's place. He let us have his bedroom. Then we met again a few days after that. I thought, to make her happy, we would stroll a little or maybe watch a film and get something to eat and then go to Abdel Hakim's. She showed up a little late and fierce as a tiger. All the masks of niceness came off. We walked for a few minutes in silence, and suddenly I felt a strong desire to go back to my room and work. I didn't want anything from her. She said she wanted to go downtown, to a place with music and dancing. I suggested we go to Abdel Hakim's place right away; she refused and asked me for 2 kopeks. Then she went to a phone booth and pulled a small notebook from her pocket. She made a call, then came back and asked for 2 more kopeks. She made another call. Was she showing me that she had other options? She said she would go downtown by herself. I left her, feeling relieved.

29

The *komendantsha* summoned me to announce that she had assigned another student to our room: a Russian. She said there were only two of us. 'Not true,' I said, 'there's Mario and Jalaleddinov.' She gave me a knowing look and didn't bother to contradict me. I spoke with the *dezhurnaya*; she looked around cautiously and whispered that some retirees would rent a room in their flat to students even though it was illegal. She gave me a nearby address, and I went there. A modern building with a lift and central heating. Above the door was a Christian icon with a little lamp. A toothless old lady lived there. One room, a kitchen and a bathroom. I didn't tell her my nationality and she didn't ask. 'Where will I sleep?' I enquired. 'Here,' she pointed to a decrepit couch. She said she would sleep in the kitchen; there was an old armchair with a pile of covers on top. I paid her 10 roubles for a month's rent. I went to the dormitory and gathered a few clothes and blankets, my typewriter and some newspapers.

30

I felt chest pain and heart palpitations. Went to the clinic. The doctor knew no English, and I couldn't explain what was wrong. I blushed and left, annoyed with myself. On the way back I was surprised to see two policemen in long military overcoats accosting me at the metro station. They grabbed my arms; I tried to protest. They didn't answer but led me brusquely to an adjacent room. There was an officer behind a desk. Next to him there was a man in his forties who looked outraged and scared. The officer asked for my ID card; I handed it over. He wrote down my information on a piece of paper and asked me to sign it. I gathered that it was a witness statement confirming what they had found when they had searched the other man: a chain of keys, an address book, a medal, a handkerchief, a pack of Russian cigarettes and some matches. These objects were piled up on the desk. I signed the statement and they let me go.

31

I knocked on the Syrians' door; Hamid opened. I asked about Zoya. He said, 'Didn't you know? She and Talia were attacked by an Azerbaijani student who beat them up and tried to rape them. He accused them of being sluts who went with foreigners. A weird thing, because he's usually a decent and gentle guy. The two girls are in the mental hospital being treated for shock. Zoya's lost her voice, and the guy got kicked out of the Institute.'

32

The *babushka*, the old lady, said she had borrowed 6 kopeks and was on her way to repay the lender. She had mentioned that to me the day before. She watched me boiling milk in the kitchen. It separated, and she said, 'You should have boiled it earlier when it was fresh.'

'You mean yesterday when I bought it?'

'Yes, of course. We're not in your country where the cows are.'

I didn't understand exactly what she meant. Perhaps she thought I was from one of the Asian Soviet republics. I had breakfast to the sound of Bach, organ variations on an Eastern melody. I called Madeleine from a phone booth in the street and tried to make a date for the next day. I said she could sleep over. She said she had planned something with friends from her university and would be staying at their place.

33

The hospital discharged Talia first. Hamid and I visited her. Books, artwork and underclothes were strewn everywhere. She had acquired two small pet birds when she got back. We talked about a teacher who always dressed too sexy because she was tired of living alone. Talia told us about the Uzbek student she was going to marry the following day. She pointed at the two birds and said they were her trousseau. We asked her about Zoya. She said she was still in the hospital and not allowed any visitors.

I picked up *Pravda*. The front page carried a picture of Brezhnev on the occasion of his receiving the Lenin Peace Prize. Talia told us a joke about him: 'So . . . he comes to his office and his private secretary says, "Comrade, one of your shoes is brown and the other is black." He replies, "I know—and would you believe it, I have another pair just like it at home!"'

She said that Brezhnev liked to collect fast new sports cars, especially American ones, and that he owned a number of them. His son owned a yacht and went hunting in Africa. And his daughter Galina liked to collect lovers and diamonds, and helped smuggle them abroad; her husband, Yuri Churbanov, the deputy minister of interior, took bribes by the millions.

34

I finished reading Yusef Khatib's *Palestine Diary*. The Palestinian as a tragic figure, the victim of conspiracies. The book quotes Churchill's speech at the British Parliament a few days before the 1917 Balfour Declaration: 'Founding a national state for the Jews in Palestine serves Britain's goals by helping her to face the sharp contradiction between her interests and those of the Arabs.' He also said: 'This Jewish state in Palestine will be a barrier dividing the Arabs to the east of Sinai from the Arabs to the west, and since it will need help defending itself against greater Arab expansion, it will always remain in the embrace of the West, which will always be able to use it as a base of operations against any challenge to the British Empire's interests in Egypt on one hand or in Iraq on the other. The Jewish state will likewise preoccupy the Arabs and absorb their energy.'*

35

I got some good work done on the newspapers, then slept for an hour. I told the *babushka* I wanted to boil some laundry. She asked me in disbelief, 'And were you planning to hang it from the balcony afterwards?'

'Why not?

'It's 1st May tomorrow—you're a Soviet citizen, do you want the Worker's Day holiday to come and have your underwear hanging out for all to see?'

She saw me heading out and asked, 'Where are you going?'

'To meet my girlfriend.'

'I know I'm alone and will always be alone.'

She stood on the threshold between the rooms until I opened the outside door, then called out, 'Bring me back some *morozhenoye*!'

I went for my date with Madeleine in front of her institute's *obshchezhitie*. One of her classmates came out to meet me, a Russian girl named Lydia. She said Madeleine had gone on a field trip to the south with the Brazilians and the rest of the Latin American students. I recalled that Mario had mentioned this. She said Madeleine had bought me a black-market ticket to the

Bolshoi Theatre for 10 roubles. She was going too; we could go together. She was slim, about my height, with prominent breasts, brown hair piled on top of her head, thin lips and a pink complexion. We went to the theatre. As I sat next to her, I could smell her greasy odour. The show was in two parts: the first was a Romantic ballet, traditional dances, boring music, except for the section where they performed Danish folk dances. But the second part was gorgeous. A ballet called *The Miraculous Mandarin*, with fast dissonant music by Béla Bartók and modern dance with nervous movements, a lot of hand gestures and acrobatic leaps.

As we were leaving the theatre, she put her hand on her head. She said she always got headaches, ever since she had separated from her husband and left her daughter in the care of her mother. A light rain started. She took a tiny umbrella out of her purse. She said she wanted to go back to the *obshchezhitie*. I said, chuckling, 'And here I was thinking we would go to my place.' She laughed, 'I can't.' We walked around Marx Prospect, then turned left and stood in front of the Sadko Cafe. She said, 'Let's have coffee here.' Then quickly withdrew, 'No, never mind. Let's go back.'

At the door of her *obshchezhitie* I asked, 'When can I see you again? Tomorrow?'

'We can't meet this week—I'm too tired, and I have to study for a big exam.'

That meant I'd have to spend the holiday weekend by myself. 'Then let's get together on Tuesday.'

'Here?'

'Anywhere else. I want to invite you over to the lion's den to celebrate your success on the exam.'

'I'm sure I won't pass.'

'Then we'll drown your sorrows with food and drink and music.'

She hesitated a little and said, 'Look, I don't know what time I'll be done, it might be seven or eight.'

'So we'll meet when you get done.'

'How about Wednesday?'

'*Khorosho*—good, 7 p.m. in front of the metro. We could go to the French embassy to see a film.'

'We'll see,' Lydia said, and we parted at the *obshchezhitie* door.

I stuck my hands in my coat pockets and walked to the end of the street. The weather was fine and warm, and the air felt fresh after the rain. I crossed a park where a number of couples were scattered on the benches, kissing. I passed a woman supporting her companion, who was talking nonstop and seemed drunk. I walked by the GUM, which carried a big red banner: 'We Are Carrying Out the Decisions of the Twenty-Fourth Party Congress.' In front of the metro was a happy-looking young Russian guy wearing trendy red bell-bottoms. He probably got them on the black market. I searched my pockets for a coin, then went down the stairs, through the passage that led to the cashier. A sign overhead urged riders to have 5 kopeks in hand before approaching the counter. I put the coin in the turnstile and waited for the little light telling me to pass. Then I took the escalator down to the lower passageway. I headed for the platform. I got on the train and stood by the door near a young blonde girl, around fifteen, who was holding hands with a boy her age. Right in front of me was a woman in her thirties who looked exhausted. After two stops, I got off at Kievskaya and took the escalator to the transfer passageway, walked along and then turned left to Turgenskaya. I took the next metro. The woman in front of me was carefully made up, with her hair arranged in rings on top of her head. The hair looked neatly done, as though she were coming straight from the hairdresser. She was sleeping. All around us were dozens of other women, their faces ordinary and unbeautiful. The driver announced: 'Exhibition Station, end of the line.' I left the metro and stood on the escalator going up. There were groups of laughing young people descending on the opposite escalator. I came out on the square and walked to the bus stop. There were colourful lights at the entrance of the Exhibition building, which had a huge, red banner with a picture of Lenin.

I stood waiting for the bus. I boarded, put 5 kopeks in the fare box and cut a ticket. I stood next to a woman who was leaning the side of her body on the back of the seat in front of her. I pressed up against her; she didn't step away. I started to get an erection, then lost the urge.

Six stops later the driver announced: 'End of the line.' He turned around in a square next to the building.

I got off the bus and went inside my building. I took the lift to the fifth floor. The flat was dark; the only glow was from the icon lamp. I opened the door and entered. The kitchen door was ajar. I thought the old woman might be at her neighbour's place watching TV. I took off my overcoat, hung it up, and took off my jacket. Then I went into the bathroom to wash my face and brush my teeth. My feet knocked over a metal bucket; I put it back in its place and dried the traces. Quietly I went into the kitchen looking for a bit of boiled potato. I saw her there, on her bed. I tiptoed back to my room and closed the door. I poured a glass of wine, took out the cellophane bag where I kept my utensils, and set out a piece of bread with cheese and olives. I lit a cigarette, then opened the window and sat there taking in the warm air. Below were three boys playing a guitar. I drank. Then I started to laugh. I drank another glass. Then I washed the plate and put it away and washed the knife and put it in the plastic bag. I lit another cigarette, then turned out the light. I got undressed and stretched out on the couch. I wrapped the covers tight around me and pulled them up over my face.

36

In the morning the old lady asked me, 'Why did you walk in on me last night?'

'I was looking for some potatoes.'

'You went out with your girlfriend and I stayed here by myself alone crying, and you didn't even bring me back any *morozhenoye*.'

'My girlfriend didn't show up.'

She smiled with delight.

I put on Bartók's 'First Piano Concerto'. The old lady came and stood in the doorway muttering in annoyance, then withdrew and turned on the radio. Military anthems. I closed the door. She opened it again, saying, 'Today is a holiday, why do you close the door on me?'

'I want to hear my music.'

'I want to hear it, too.'

'You're the one who turned on the radio so I couldn't listen.'

'I'll turn it off now.'

And she went and switched off the radio. Then her neighbour arrived, and they shut the door on me.

I worked on the newspapers for a while, then the sun came out. I stood at the window. People in their holiday clothes and children carrying balloons. Men carrying bags of bananas, provided for purchase on holidays. I saw Zoya walking arm in arm with a man with a buzz cut: probably her husband. A chubby man, slightly taller than her, wearing specs, walking beside her with very erect posture; he looked ridiculous. They passed my building walking towards the bus stop. She walked absently, lost in thought. It was the first time I had seen her since she went to the hospital. Then I noticed a blonde I had met in the lift, who seemed very shy. She was sitting on a stone bench by the door, dressed up nicely, with her daughter beside her.

A little later I went to the kitchen to make coffee. I found the old woman stretched out on her bed. She was sobbing, 'You have everything. I don't have anyone to help me. No one needs me. I'm going to end it all with the kitchen knife.'

I sat beside her. 'Why don't you go out, take a walk down the street to the cinema?'

'I don't feel like it. On a holiday like this I would have loved to go out to the country or anywhere at all, but I'm not going to go by myself like an idiot, no, I won't.'

'But you have your friend.'

She corrected me, 'My neighbour, not my friend. My friend is dead.'

'It doesn't matter.'

'But she has her daughter and granddaughter. I was just over there with them, but then some guests came, and they're all together around the table now. I don't have anyone at all. No husband, no family, no grandkids.'

She asked me to buy *morozhenoye* for her and the neighbour, and handed me 40 kopeks. I got dressed and went outside. I went to the shop and bought half a loaf of bread and a bottle of *kefir*. Then I looked for the *morozhenoye* vendor and finally found him.

I ran into Hamid. He said he had just woken up and found Farid and Sharif gone; they must be at the Workers' Day demonstration, which would carry on until 2 p.m. 'They've left me stranded. What am I supposed to do now?'

I invited him over: 'We'll have something to eat, then we'll see.'

'What are you having?'

'Boiled potatoes, because of my stomach.'

'And let's fry some eggs.'

'OK, I have some eggs.' We went to a vegetable shop too, but found only a jar of sweet pickles.

Hamid told me that the day before he had gone with the Sudanese guy Hassan and a girl he had with him to Aragvi, the best Georgian restaurant in Moscow. They had feasted on Armenian brandy and grilled chicken with *tsatsivi* sauce, fresh tomatoes, sauerkraut and red peppers. Although Hassan was playing the host, he had refused to pay, sticking Hamid with a tab of 25 roubles instead, even though he was sure the Sudanese had plenty of money on him.

I asked him about Zoya. He said she was out of the hospital and staying with her family. The day before, she had come over to his room and brought her husband along, and they had all hung out together without incident. I said that was bad; she shouldn't put him in a position like that, when everyone knows she's been cheating on him.

We walked towards my place. Hamid asked, 'Don't you think I have the right to ask the Sudanese guy for my money?' I nodded, 'Of course.'

He recalled an incident: 'One time I went into a restaurant with a girl, thinking I had 6 roubles with me, and she must have at least 5. We drank a bottle of vodka, and then I put my hand in my pocket and found just 1 miserable rouble. I asked how much she had and it was just a few kopeks. I didn't know what to do, so I took off a gold chain that I had bought in West Germany for 30 marks, that is, 40 roubles. I called over the waiter and asked, "Does this appeal?" He nodded and quickly took away the chain. "Then bring us another bottle of vodka." He did and disappeared for a while, then reappeared, dropped the chain on the table and said no, it didn't appeal after all. What to do? I looked all around the restaurant in confusion, when suddenly a man with Eastern-looking features came up to us and paid our bill. He introduced himself as an oil engineer from

Baku, the capital of Azerbaijan, and when I insisted he sat down and joined us.'

'Strange, these Azerbaijanis—where do they get money? How much does he get a month?'

'About 200 roubles.'

'That's not enough for anything but their idiotic hospitality.'

'But they have other sources of income—the black market. No one lives on his salary. That's true of all the republics but especially the Asian ones. I had a friend from Uzbekistan—you wouldn't believe the stuff he told me about the corruption there. Some people live like in the Middle Ages, with private armies, militias. Ordinary workers are like serfs in their fiefdom.'

We went to my room. The old woman was playing cards with the neighbour and another old woman. I gave her the *morozhenoye*. Then I gave her a copy of *The Last Knight*, and said, 'Reading is good.' The neighbour approved, 'Great. That's a lovely novel.' The old woman said, 'Better than crying, anyway.'

Hamid took a seat in my room. I brought a tin of meat, four eggs, a bottle of Algerian red wine and a can of boiled cauliflower. I told him I was uncomfortable opening the tin in the kitchen; it costs a rouble, and these old ladies live on kopeks. I went to the kitchen a number of times and turned around, confused; then I went one more time, walked to the cabinet and took the can-and-bottle opener. The old woman stared at me with childlike curiosity. I went back to the room and gave the opener to Hamid. He attached it to the can on the table and hit it with his hand; the table made a sound. I hissed, shh. I thought I heard the old woman snarl. I took the can from him and put it on the wood floor. I hit the opener with my hand, then he continued the job, being careful not to make a sound, until it opened.

I carried the tin back to the kitchen and looked for the big saucepan with the handle, while the old woman, still playing cards, watched me closely. I asked her for the saucepan; she said, 'I'm using it for my food. Take the small one.' I muttered that the small one wasn't big enough, and where was it, anyway.

'I don't know, look around.'

I opened the cabinet again and found it on the bottom shelf. I put the can on the stove and rinsed the saucepan. I noticed the meat peeking out of the can, so I hurried to transfer it into the tiny saucepan; it almost spilt over. The other old woman said, 'Give him the big saucepan, that one's too small.' I gathered my courage and told her firmly, 'Please give me the larger saucepan.'

She looked at me, agitated.

I assured her, 'I'll move its contents into another vessel, then put it back.'

'Where? It's my saucepan and my potatoes.'

Then she got up. Brought the big pan and emptied it into another container, fuming, 'Go buy yourself a saucepan. This is my pan and these are my potatoes.' The other old women sat silently; after a while they left.

She washed the pan herself, wiped it with the filthy rag and handed it to me. I moved the contents of the smaller pan into it while she continued to circle around me, snarling with irritation. Then I broke the four eggs in the pan and carried it to the table. She went into my room and walked all around it, then came out and offered us her two old forks that looked like filthy fox claws. I put them aside and took two forks out of my cellophane bag.

I opened the bottle of wine, but the cork fell apart. I said, 'Must be a Soviet cork.' Hamid nodded, 'Of course—it's bottled here. They import the wine from Algeria in barrels or tanker ships.' We drank some and gagged a little, it was so bitter. He said, 'The Algerians sell their decent wine to France and send the other stuff here.'

'They must add water to it here.'

'And other junk. Look what's in the bottom of the glass. Have you seen the film, *Listopad*, about a wine factory where they water down the wine to meet their production quota?' I didn't remember. He continued, 'It's a satire by Iosseliani, same guy who did *Once Upon a Time There Was a Singing Blackbird*. There's this young, honest guy who gets a job in a wine factory where everyone's a cheat. He discovers that the wine is watered down and everyone tells him there's no point telling on the boss. Then this girl from the factory flirts with him, lures him home, and in front of her house he's beaten up by this thug who's her boyfriend while she looks on. Then he goes back to the factory with his bruised-up face, meets the girl, who tries to apologize, but he just pats her cheek, says, "It's nothing, girl," then brushes her off as she tries to follow him. Then he goes and orders the workers to stop pumping the wine and asks them to pour some kind of tar into the tank where they water it down, and announces that no one will be able to tamper with the wine now.'

We finished the bottle and each lit a cigarette. The old lady appeared, complaining, 'Too much smoke. I have a headache. Why don't you smoke on the balcony?'

I replied, angrily, 'Don't come in the room. I'm going to smoke here.'

'This is my home, I'll come in where I want.'

'I'll close the door.' I was about to close it but she stopped me irritably, her face reddening. 'Then I'll move out,' I declared.

'Fine.'

I sat with Hamid as he fought back laughter. 'Old people, old people! . . . Let's go out.'

'Where do you want to go?' I asked.

'Anywhere there's beer. Today's a holiday and there's no point spending it here.'

I told him how the old woman had quietly opened the door of my room at night while I was asleep; when I woke up and asked what she wanted, she didn't say anything, so I asked again, and then she told me she just wanted some medicine, but that I should go back to sleep and not keep awake.

Hamid said, 'I used to live with an old lady who was a lot of fun. She was clean and strong, and she used to laugh with me and ask me about what girls were like in bed, and she recorded all my phone calls. But this one is pathetic.'

The old woman started looking for her housekey; she wanted to go out but couldn't remember where she had put it. Hamid said to me, 'Don't worry about it, that's how old people are. Next she'll blame the cigarette smoke.' After a while, she found her key and went out.

He resumed, 'There's no point spending the day here. Let's go out and drink some beer.' I told him I wasn't supposed to drink a lot, and I planned to work later anyway. He said, 'You know what I want right now? A woman.'

'Me too.'

'Let's go look for some.'

'Where?'

'Downtown.'

I asked about his girlfriend Tania. He told me about their problems: he had been in a car with Tania, drunk, and had kissed her friend the ballet dancer, so she had stormed out of the car angrily and fallen down on the ground and said she never wanted to see him again.

'Was the friend pretty?' I asked.

'Her body was amazing.'

'So stay with her.'

'But I want Tania.'

'What about your wife?' I smirked.

'She's in Damascus.'

The wife came from a prominent family. Hamid had met her at a sports club, and when his scholarship to Russia had come through, he had decided to marry her and get her pregnant before he went abroad. I asked why. He said in order to keep her busy in his absence and to make sure she didn't leave him.

I put on a blue turtleneck sweater and a blue jacket over it. We got on the bus, then the metro, and sat at the very back of the last car. In front of us was a woman of about forty-five, with a dull complexion. Her lips were rouged and her hair was loose and falling over her forehead. She was wearing a brand-new summer jacket and new shoes. Her hand, which had no wedding ring, was closed around a purse on top of which lay a folded magazine and a small umbrella. She was looking down and avoided raising her eyes in any direction.

I said to Hamid, 'She's going to read a foreign literary magazine and go to the ballet or the theatre. All she wants is a man, but the men are all drunk.'

He observed, 'You know how many people live in Moscow? Between 8 and 10 million. Let's say a million of them are married, and 2 million are old folks past the age of having sex, and another 2 million are old people but still able to have sex, and 3 million are women between the age of 20 and 45.' A moment later he added, 'And they're all living off small triumphs—buying flowers during a snowstorm in February, getting their hands on a pair of theatre tickets, finding a pair of shoes their size or some imported German panties on sale at the Leipzig shop.'

We got off at Lenin Library Station. We took the underground passage to another stop and from there to the beer bar—it was closed. We leant against the wall and watched the thousands of people coming and going past us.

Hamid said, 'Where should we go?'

'I don't know—you're the leader.'

We went to Cafe Elite. It was packed. We stood next to two girls. One glanced at me; I smiled. One of them was very beautiful, the other very ugly. Hamid pulled me by the arm and said, 'That's a *nabor*.'

'What do you mean?'

'A rule of Soviet life. When you want to buy something, you find it's bundled with something else that you don't want at all, and you have to buy them together. Should we go in?'

'I don't know.'

He looked around, dissuaded, 'There's no room.'

'What about downstairs?'

'Forget it, let's go.'

We walked down to the end of the street, towards Arbat, the grand restaurant, which consisted of an enormous room with rows of tables and chairs. The window showed three female singers on a stage. An astonishing number of women were sitting by themselves. When we got to the entrance, we saw a guard standing between the people and the door. Hamid pushed me ahead of him, saying I looked foreign. The guard stopped me; I told him we were going to the bar. He waved us in and we went into the bar, a long room full of tables, with a plate-glass window looking out on the street.

There were some empty seats by the bar, but it was all men. We chose a table where a young woman was already sitting with a young man leaning towards her. We asked, 'Are the two chairs *svobodni*—free?' He said yes. We sat down, and Hamid asked me what we should drink. 'You're the leader,' I repeated. He went to the bar. I felt the young woman looking at me. I glanced at the neighbouring table: there were three girls, one ugly, one with her back to me, and the third of average prettiness. I saw two guys come over to them and stand there talking, in what seemed like an invitation; the girls laughed and turned them down. Hamid returned with two tall glasses: some kind of cocktail, a mixture of gin and vodka and cognac, with cherries and a slice of pear at the bottom. We sat sucking the frozen liquid through straws.

Our neighbour was petite, moderately pretty, wearing a short elegant dress. The young man was wearing a colourful tie over a new shirt whose sleeves protruded from a jacket decorated with large beige glass buttons. He was talking with his hand on his cheek; their conversation was intermittent. I heard her say, playfully, '*Ya ne mogu*—I can't.' Fireworks went off in the sky; the young woman turned on her round stool, her thighs facing me, to watch the sky through the sheet of glass. I noticed that she was looking more at her own reflection in the glass than at the sky. A fat old lady dressed like a worker came and pulled the curtains on the big window, and said irritably, 'Not allowed.' I told her we wanted to watch the fireworks display. She snapped, 'Go watch at home or on the streets. Here, no.' Our neighbour took this opportunity to engage us in conversation, expressing her displeasure at this stupidity.

'It must be that today is a holiday and she's alone,' I said.

'Very likely. We're here to have a good time, but she's dumb and horrible.'

The guy turned red and chided her, 'You'd do better to focus on your drink.' I got up and pulled back the curtain; the girl cheered. The old woman came and closed the curtain again, yelling angrily, and cursed at the girl. Soon I heard her complaining she was bored; the boy suggested they leave. She got up and said goodbye to us, the boy moving in silence, looking down at the floor, blood rising in his face. I wished him, '*S prazd-nikom*, happy holiday.' He answered, '*S prazdnikom.*'

I turned my attention to the next table. There was a tall, wide man in spectacles with his back to me. Beside him, a trim young woman with yellow-highlighted ringlets, soft rouge-pink lips and false eyelashes. Her short dress showed her thighs in white tights.

I said to Hamid, 'A bureaucrat with his secretary.'

'Or a big Party member.'

There was a long silence between the man and the woman. He would sometimes break it; she would listen to him and then slap on his arm playfully. She noticed that I was watching and wiped her eyes, then looked down at her thighs, making no attempt to hide them.

Hamid said, 'Let's go.'

'Let's stay.'

'Come on, let's get out of here.'

'To where?'

He suggested we go to the bar called Green, or Luxor—we'd meet Finnish and Danish girls there. We walked out into the street and made our way through the crowd. I looked at the tall buildings of Kalinin Street, full of flowers and red banners and posters proclaiming: 'Glory to May 1' and 'Glory to Work.' Hamid remarked, 'Yesterday I got drunk with Sharif and Farid and we got into a long argument about Marxism-Leninism, each of us claiming to be more Marxist-Leninist than the other.'

At the metro station, a slogan spelt out in coloured lights: 'Glory to the Communist Party.' And above it, a news ticker in lights: 'Respected Citizens of Moscow, Come Watch the Film, *Fifty Years of the Soviet Union*.' Red Square was bright with lights and red banners. As we turned onto Gorky Street, which sloped up gradually, we were met by a huge crowd of people heading down to the square singing patriotic hymns and songs.

We went into a hotel and headed up to the bar; it charged in dollars and looked like a cave. In shaky English Hamid ordered two whiskies. I looked at him curiously, and he whispered, 'If I had ordered in Russian, he would have stiffed us.' The bar was full of foreigners and Soviets from the Asian republics. He said, 'Secret deals are made here—timber smuggled to Central Asia, black caviar shipped to the West in tins labelled "Herring", gold and furs and diamonds, icons, even imported birth-control pills.'

A dark, handsome young man sat across from us. He asked me, 'Where from?'

'Egypt.'

He said he was from Mexico and laughed, 'Is Fatah still a thing, or is it all over?'

'That is the question.'

The girl with him was Russian, with extremely thin eyebrows and a hand on her cheek. They chatted haltingly. A bearded guy joined them, and then another group—two young men, one Finnish or German and the other American- or British-looking, also bearded, and a slim Russian girl. A chortling chatterbox who couldn't stop hugging the German guy. And next to me, an old woman with a young man who looked Somali or Ethiopian: he brought two drinks and started kissing her; I heard her say she wanted to take his photo. Then a tall blonde young woman with a handsome Kirghiz, who held her hand to his cheek as he closed his eyes affectionately; she, like a queen, let him kiss her hand; we discovered her face was plain.

We were joined by a woman in her forties who ordered a bottle of wine. Hamid told her, 'Let's drink to your birthday.' We drank. She tried to talk to us, but we ignored her. She finished the bottle, shaking her head in sad resignation, and left.

A clamorous group of tourists arrived, led by a tall woman in red who had her arm around another woman. From behind us came the sound of dance music. A tall slim girl in cowboy pants, with a prominent nose, approached and said to the bearded American, 'I want a drink.' He seemed to know her but was not thrilled at her arrival. She sat down next to him on the same chair, and I heard her telling someone else that she was Jewish.

Hamid said, 'Let's go.' It was already midnight, but the streets were still crowded. Outside the metro station there was a young man dressed as a woman. He had put some bits of clothing over his chest and backside and was shaking them. Some people gathered around him to watch.

37

The old woman chided me for not saying good morning. She asked me to put on whatever music I liked. I got some good work done. Then I left the room.

She asked me, 'Don't you want some tea?'

'Yes, of course.' I followed her to the kitchen. I put a spoonful of tea into my plastic mug.

I turned on the stove but, as usual, she said, 'The water in the kettle is hot already.'

'But I want it boiling.'

As I had expected, she said, 'It just boiled.'

'No, it should be boiling when I add it to the tea.'

'Do what you want.'

Her breath smelt terrible, as did her body; her face was red. 'I have a headache,' she said.

'The sun is scorching today.'

'I was at the cemetery. There were a lot of people and the sun was beating down. I brought a broom along and cleaned up the grave, then I put some flowers on it.' She smiled and added, 'His gravestone is nice. It's green and grey. I can't complain.' A tear welled up in her eye. 'Next time I'll buy some paints and decorate the grave, cheer it up a little. He's in the dark now.'

In the street I met Zoya and her husband. She kissed me on the cheek and introduced me, 'This is the one I told you about.' She asked if Hans was back. I ignored the question. We stopped by the house of a friend of hers, who came out to meet us after we called to her.

She asked Zoya's husband, 'When did you get here?' And then, with a laugh, 'When are you leaving?'

38

The newspapers announced that the Lebanese Army was wiping out the Palestinian guerrillas in Lebanon. Hans returned from Germany. We went together to the nearby 'Exhibition of Achievements of the National Economy of the Soviet Union'. It rained lightly. We walked in past the giant steel statue of a young man holding up a hammer and a woman raising a sickle and striding boldly towards the dawning future. Across it was the big steel replica of the *Vostok* in which Gagarin had flown into space; one side of it had a painting of several scientists and engineers boarding him onto the capsule, and the other had Lenin leading the masses into space. We walked through the nuclear energy wing and other wings devoted to the coal industry, biology, education, physics, trade unions, electrical technology and agriculture. Hans said East Germany looked a lot like Russia, but people were more disciplined. I asked him about his family back home; he said his mother was unhappy with the doctor she had married after his father had disappeared during the war—he was a vicious man who had been cruel to Hans, and had eventually abandoned them. I told him about my mother, who was paralysed.

We approached the mock space-capsules that hold two people, zoom up in the air and swivel. Hans suggested we try one. I refused. He bought two tickets. We noticed a tall girl in a coat and black trousers sitting on a bench. She had wide blue eyes and a long face framed by straight black hair, and a full sensuous mouth. He said to her, holding up the tickets, 'Come with me.' She blushed and said she had been up already. He went up to her, sat down next to her, and bummed a cigarette. People passing or sitting nearby were looking at us. I sat on another chair near two girls and offered them the tickets, but they said they were scared and laughed shyly. One of them asked me where we were from. All the time they were looking at Hans. He went up in the ride with the blue-eyed brunette. They spun in the air, shrieking and laughing. When they came back down, she had held his arm. After a while she let go of him and walked by his side. We went to the ride with rectangular capsules that spin fast and gradually rise. We wanted to buy tickets but found the window closed. One of the workers told us that the ride was still open for another hour, but the ticket seller's shift had ended. They let us in without tickets. We went up in the box and lay supine staring at the sky. She put her hand on Hans' arm again when we got down. On our bus ride home she sat next to a stranger who asked her about me. She told him I was an Arab. Hans whispered, 'She guessed from your accent without me telling her—she must have some experience. She works at a store, and she's married.' I left them by my house. A terrible headache battered me all night long. I felt it hitting my eye, moving upward and then hitting the backside of my neck. I woke the old woman; she gave me a painkiller.

39

'It's Sunday and the sun is shining—aren't you going out?' the old woman asked.

'I don't feel like it.'

'You're like me—tired of life.'

I drank tea, thinking about the face of the girl at the exhibition. The wide blue eyes, the cheeks framed by long smooth hair, the sensuous lips. I read an article on Cervantes. His biography was quite like *Don Quixote*. In his youth he had suffered a nervous breakdown linked to acute religiosity.

I went out to the nearby cinema. They were screening *Free Birds*. A Bulgarian coming-of-age story. One scene brought tears to my eyes—the adolescent was with a woman, staring at her legs.

Madeleine came over in a taxi. She was late. The old woman welcomed her warmly. When we were alone, I said. 'You deserve a beating.' She took off her clothes, and asked, 'Are you going to beat me?' She was clean and neat and smelt of nothing. She said, 'Do you love me just a little bit?' It took some effort to get inside.

I came with a violent whole-body shudder. She brought her hand up to her ear, and I complimented her earring. It was Mario's, she told me.

40

Hans gave me an old issue of *Literaturnaya Gazeta* featuring several poems by the dissident poet Yevgeny Yevtushenko, entitled 'Dispatch from the Continent of Hope'.* He said the authorities had finally accepted the poet, or perhaps he had made peace with the authorities. Yevtushenko was appointed as special literary correspondent to the newspaper and now spent several months a year in Latin America, travelling from country to country.

41

It rained incessantly. The room was cold since the heating was turned off according to the calendar. I put the lamp up high so Zoya could see I was in if she decided to stop by. After two hours I turned off the light and lay down. I tucked myself in carefully; a few tosses and turns to adjust to the hills and valleys of the couch. I dreamt uneasy dreams about my father. For the first time I saw him alive, elegantly dressed, going to visit a woman in Europe. I left him a note asking him to bring me back the biggest collection of detective novels he could find.

Next morning, the old woman opened the door on me early. I snarled. She said she was worried that I had left without paying the rent and the electricity bill; she had found one of her previous tenants sleeping with his head on his suitcase, preparing to leave without paying his dues. I said sharply, 'You could have waited till I woke up.' She shouted back saying she was free to do what she pleased; she just wanted to breathe. Then she walked into her room, opened a shabby cabinet and began counting the chipped old dishes.

42

We had dinner at a restaurant—Hans and I, Madeleine and Isadora. The latter mentioned that she had broken up with her Brazilian boyfriend. Two days later we saw each other again; we met at 10 p.m. and went straight to my room. The old woman welcomed us, smiling. I told her my friends were staying over, so she gave me an extra pillow and two more blankets. I spread a blanket in the corner for Hans and Isadora; Madeleine and I slept on the couch.

I followed the sounds coming from the floor and announced, jokingly, that I was going to join them. I sat up. Madeleine grabbed my arm and looked like she was about to cry. Isadora warned me to stay away. In the morning she looked grim, and Hans seemed embarrassed. The old woman was out somewhere. He and I stood in the kitchen after breakfast. He whispered, 'In the middle of it, she shook me and asked, "You call this sex?"' He added, 'My sexual experience was really lacking until I met her. German and Russian girls are just glad and grateful for any sexual attention you want to give them, but these Latin Americans?

They'll practically tear you limb from limb if they don't get an orgasm. They'll just come right out and tell you—I'm not satisfied.'

43

After her husband went back to his unit, Zoya moved out of her mother's house and back into the *obshchezhi-tie*. We celebrated her birthday. She was alone when I went to give her a present—a Pharaonic bracelet. She told me how the Azerbaijani guy had tried to rape her, yelling that she always gave herself to Hans easily. When she tried to push him away, he started hitting her, and when Talia came to her rescue he beat her up, too. I told her I was sorry, and she said she felt sure that I loved her. She was a little tipsy and flushed; I felt a very strong desire to hold her and kiss her. I put my hand on her head and smoothed her hair. She said she didn't love Hans any more, because she had realized that he didn't really need her, and because he got angry once when she was late for a date with him and accused her of being with Vladimir—that drunk.

44

The old lady seemed to be in a fine mood. She said it was finally her turn in the government queue for a better flat; I should get ready to move out. She was sitting in her usual place by the stove. I teased her but she frowned, saying she had to focus on planning.

Madeleine had promised she would come at 1 p.m. I went out, not wearing my *shapka*, and bought meat and beer. I cleaned my room. Waited for her until four. Zoya had also promised me, two days ago, that she would stop by this evening. I sat down to work, looking out the window and waiting for her. But she didn't come either. My prostate still hurt whenever I got aroused.

45

I went to the *obshchezhitie* to pick up some newspapers.
I ran into Hans. He asked me whether Zoya had come
to visit me.

I called up Madeleine and invited her over. I made
a salad and opened a bottle of Bulgarian red wine. I put
on a record of Rimsky-Korsakov's Russian Easter Festival Overture—exhilarating music, its insistent percus-
sion rhythm beginning soft and slow and building to a
joyous climax with other instruments and Eastern
melodies. This time Madeleine came, but she was not
in the mood for lovemaking. She said, with a nasty look,
'I had an abortion.'

I gaped at her dumbfounded, 'Why didn't you tell
me?'

'Because it wasn't yours.'

'Whose, then?'

'Mario,' she said, and waited for some reaction,
but I was silent. She told me how one of her Russian
classmates had taken her secretly to somebody's flat
for the abortion. The operating table had been a bed in
the living room. A few days later she had started to
haemorrhage and had to go to the same place by

herself; to her surprise the bed had disappeared and the room was filled with normal flat stuff. I was stunned. She said there were underground groups who did abortions secretly. Abortion was legal, but only in hospitals; yet many women couldn't go because they didn't want their families or workplaces to know. If the director of Madeleine's institute found out, they would deport her. She then wrapped her arms around me and asked, 'Aren't you going to beat me?' She rubbed herself against my leg to a powerful orgasm.

46

Zoya stopped by at 9 p.m. She seemed tired. She thanked me again for the bracelet and kissed me on both cheeks. She rubbed her forehead with her fingers to wipe off any dust specks. I offered her a drink, some wine or vodka. She looked at me cannily, tucking a curl behind her ear, and asked, 'What for?' I kept moving around the whole time, standing or sitting, while she sat and watched my every move as though expecting something. I helped her review her English homework. At midnight she announced she wanted to leave. I said, 'It's late. I'll walk you. Where are you spending the night?'

'In the *obshchezhitie*.'

'Is it still open?'

'I'll get in.'

'If you can't, then please come back here.'

I walked her to the lift. She kept watching me from the corner of her eye as though at any moment she expected me to make a pass at her.

47

Madeleine called at 6 p.m., as expected. She said, 'I know you don't want to see me—I'm no good right now after the operation.' We agreed to meet in front of the Bolshoi. I took her to Abdel Hakim's place. His wife wasn't back from Ukraine yet. Their marriage seemed to be on the rocks. We hung out drinking with him and the two women he had over: a heavy-lipped colleague named Emma and a tall young girl who spoke good English and talked continuously, quickly, breathlessly —her name was Larissa; I had met her back in Cairo, at a bookstore. Abdel Hakim took me to the kitchen and warned me that Emma had ties to the KGB. He told us Gaddafi had just nationalized an American oil company and announced Libya's diplomatic recognition of East Germany. We talked ironically about the Third Way theory, which opposed both capitalism and what it called reactionary communists who clung to the rigid moulds of the past. When we got drunk, he suggested a game where each woman would choose a number representing the two of us and spend some time alone with the winner. I won twice. I took Emma to the kitchen and kissed her on the mouth. She returned the kiss fervently, so I pressed my leg against her. Then I did likewise with Larissa who was quite cross because I had not called her since the last time we met. We returned to the living room and I suggested, laughing, that we try group sex. We all laughed, but Madeleine got upset and disappeared in the bathroom. Then the two women left.

I spent the night on the living-room couch with Madeleine. I could smell a stink just from lying down next to her. She admitted that she hadn't cleaned herself after using the toilet because she couldn't find any paper.

'Wasn't there any water?'

'Of course. There was a bottle there, but I don't know how to use it like you guys do.'

I turned my back to her and slept.

48

I called Larissa; her mother answered the phone. She said in a feeble voice that her daughter had told her about me. She asked me to take good care of her. She gave her the receiver, and we agreed to meet downtown. She arrived twenty minutes late, just as I was about to leave. I recalled that she was always late in Cairo, too, and would make excuses about escaping the surveillance at the embassy. She was wearing a short chequered red skirt that showed off her pretty legs, full buttocks and narrow waist. We walked down Kalinin Prospect. She asked breathlessly, 'Where to?'

'Let's buy some food and go to my place.'

'Tell me about the old lady—when you said on the phone you had rented a room from an old lady, I wanted to know what sort of old lady she was.' After a moment she said, 'Wouldn't it be better for us to go out someplace, a cafe or a restaurant?'

I considered it. Good food and drink, but she would give me a headache with her chatter and after that it would be too late to go to my room, and I'd be out 10 to 12 roubles. I said, 'As you please—we'll see.'

'Remember the last time we went out, we had dinner and then you refused to escort me home?'

'That was because I had only had 10 roubles in my pocket, and I had spent all of it.'

We got into a long conversation about health, neurosis and sex—primitive customs, female frigidity, Lady Chatterley, the shell of civilization that makes the sexual encounter difficult and complicated, the promiscuous man—I said either he was looking to match the ideal image in his head, or he was a closet homosexual. She explained that love was a culmination or a refinement of the sexual encounter, and that was the goal of communism as well. I asked about her Armenian boyfriend. She said she had broken up with him; he was a little tyrant and expected a woman to do what he wanted. I said, 'And why not, if the sex is good?' She said, impassively, 'Of course, but it wasn't—he was so selfish, he only cared about his own pleasure.' I asked about her friend Olga, whom I had also met in Cairo. She was tiny and pale. Yet she had been surrounded by Egyptian guys all the time. Larissa said Olga had been confused ever since she had returned from Egypt: no one paid her any attention here or took her out anywhere; she spent all her time in her room, sleeping. We recalled Svetlana, her other friend. She had an elegant figure and a high bust, and she used to go around with her head held high, proud and beautiful. She said, 'You wouldn't recognize her now. She married a Russian and has two children. She's gained a lot of weight, and always seems full of tears—her husband beats her.'

'Let's go eat at Moskva, if you have money,' she said.

'How much will it cost?'

'10 or 15 roubles.'

'I can't.'

I bought a bottle of Bulgarian red wine for 180 kopeks and a chunk of *kolbasa* stuffed with egg, as well as some cold beef. We went to my place. She said, 'You'll escort me home when I leave.'

'Why?'

She replied, in English, '*That is a gentleman's duty.*'

'I don't care about that stuff.'

'Why?'

'It doesn't make any sense for me to take you from one end of the city to the other, then turn around and come back. We both work in the morning.'

She said it was a rather mundane issue. Then she said, 'In that case I won't stay long. I'll leave before ten.'

'As you wish.'

We stopped by the *obshchezhitie* to get fresh linen and then went to the flat. The old woman was in the kitchen with another old woman who wore spectacles. I set the table, avoiding going to the kitchen. Then I put two pieces of meat on one of her old plates and brought it to them; the old lady was happy. Her friend asked, 'Do you have anything to drink?' I poured her a glass of wine. I returned to Larissa and we began eating and drinking. The old woman came and said she would kick her friend out and go to bed. She then closed the door on us. Larissa said she hated old people like her, 'They're like dogs—you feed them and they shut up.' Her father was pathetic too, he would close the windows and ask about everything: Why is this standing here? Why there? He was an animal. I asked what he did for a living. She said he was a crewman on big ships, always away and then he'd return and get her mother pregnant and leave her struggling with eight children—he'd ruined her life.

'How?'

'My mother never got any sexual satisfaction, but because she's religious, she could never have a relationship with anyone besides her husband.' She said she was very close to her mother and hated her father and wished he would die.

We finished the food, and she said she was going. I said, 'It would be better for you to stay and spend the night with me—most likely nothing will happen.' She didn't object but said her mother would be waiting up for her. We went down to call her from the kiosk. She spoke in a sweet voice into the phone, '*Mamochka*, I'm spending the night at my girlfriend's. How are you doing?' She listened for a moment, then worriedly asked, 'Oh, is it Dad again?'

We went back upstairs. I closed the bedroom door, went to the bathroom and undressed. The old lady opened the door in a ragged undershirt. She yelled, 'Are you having her spend the night?'

I said, confused, 'I don't understand.'

'I'm going to tell your girlfriend everything.'

After she went away we lay down on the couch. She undressed. I found her very wet, entered her easily and finished quickly. Just as I was falling asleep, with the taste of her greasy lips still on mine, I felt her fingers trying to stir me to life again, with no result. In the morning her fingers repeated the effort, again without success. I showered and got dressed while she examined her naked body with a strange wonder. She would take one pose after another and ask me what I thought of her body. I said it was beautiful.

I accompanied her on the bus to the metro station. She asked me if I or any of my friends could buy her tickets to the American concert.

I promised to call her, certain that I wouldn't.

49

It was time to move out of the old woman's house and return to the *obshchezhitie*. I was expecting a battle: that the old woman would steal something from me or accuse me of stealing something from her, or try to extort money from me. At the very least, to replace the plastic tablecloth I had torn. But she didn't do any of that, didn't even peek into the things I had packed. She asked for 50 kopeks to cover the electricity bill; she could have asked for a whole rouble. We said goodbye, and she said she was sorry to see me go; I was a good person. I moved back into my old room at the *obshchezhitie*. The Russian student welcomed me. He had a sturdy build and a military-style crew cut. Mario wasn't there.

50

Zoya was back in hospital, and I went to visit her with Hans. She paid attention only to him. She said how she wished one of us would visit her sometime and take her for a walk outside the hospital, as her husband used to do.

After we left her, we walked in the sunset glow. The weather was pleasant—it reminded me of winter in Cairo. Hans said Farid and Hamid had moved out of the *obshchezhitie* into a private flat and that he had the room to himself now; he invited me to move in, and added, 'We have two desks, one for each of us.' I agreed.

I moved all my stuff to his room. I claimed the bed to the left of the window. We dismantled the third bed and put it on top of the wooden wardrobe. We agreed to pool our shopping and split the expenses. I ran into Mario in the hallway. We walked down to the cafeteria together. He seemed embarrassed, but I spoke with him casually. We stood in the queue. He suddenly said that Madeleine loved us both—each of us satisfied a different thing—he was like her brother and I was like her father.

51

Hans returned at midnight, annoyed. He said the Russian teacher Tatiana—blonde, fortyish, heavy, bespectacled—had invited him to her house at 4 p.m., saying she'd cooked two ducks, Russian-style. He arrived late because he was out with Isadora. He finally got there at ten, and found her sitting in front of the cold food, waiting along with other guests. As though he were some kind of VIP, everything was held up until he arrived, as a result the dinner was ruined, the teacher sulked the whole time; he stayed only for a little while.

'You should have visited Zoya,' I said.

'I didn't feel like seeing her.'

52

I went to the Egyptian embassy at Khlebny Street to fill out some paperwork. A tall man met me at the premises, but paid no attention to me. He turned to a large map of the USSR on the wall, looking for a point. After a moment, he spoke: 'They've abandoned us.'

I disagreed. 'Not true. What were they supposed to do besides rebuild the Egyptian Army?'

'They don't want us to fight to recover our lands.'

'No, they just don't want us to risk a war, badly prepared as we are, and make a mess of it—look at our record.'

He looked at me for a long time without answering.

While walking back to the metro I noticed a strongly built woman with fantastic breasts and a complexion like the sun: I desired her almost to the point of tears. I saw another woman with a big derrière jamming herself into the crowd and turning down an available seat. She was wearing a wedding ring. I followed her as she got off the train. I realized that she was looking for someone to rub against her. She hurried into the crowd by the escalator, with me behind her. She rode it down to the lower train and boarded, looking around awkwardly, then went by the door where some passengers had clustered. I left her and went on my way.

53

Hans tidied the room, and we made supper. Sharif and Hamid, the Syrians, came over with a bottle of vodka to celebrate Farid's graduation. Sharif mentioned that Gaddafi had announced he was secluding himself to meditate. Also that al-Bakr, the representative of the Ba'ath party in Iraq, had signed an agreement with Aziz Muhammad, the secretary of the Iraqi Communist Party, to form the National Progressive Front. Hamid said they would probably just take advantage of the agreement to gather intelligence on the communists, then start a crackdown. Sharif spoke about his girl, Marina, who had to perform abortions on herself because she had no residence permit and therefore couldn't access a hospital, leaving her no other choice except a clandestine operation which would cost money. He said she used a suction bulb to draw out the blood; once he had woken up to find her face turning blue. Hamid said he had once asked his girlfriend to leave the room so that another girl could come over; she had refused and threatened to kill herself. He'd said to her then, 'Go ahead, kill yourself.' She went to the bathroom while he sat down to drink vodka. Fifteen minutes passed, she still hadn't come out. Then after half an hour she appeared, all pale, and said she was dying and collapsed on the bed. He called an ambulance. Three people came, a female doctor and a nurse and a driver; they saved her, then they all sat down to drink vodka and chat. Then Hamid announced that he was going to Damascus soon; he missed his wife and daughter. He showed us their picture. Later, we were joined by Irma, her eyes red from crying. They left when the vodka bottle was near empty. As I was cleaning the room, Hind came in. She said she had run into Sharif and Hamid on the stairs and knew what they were saying about her because of her relationship with the Russian student. I asked if she loved him.

'I don't know.'

'You can gauge by the physical intimacy.'

'It's tough in our conditions—I've got roommates and so has he. I know there must be other ways to have sex besides me lying on my back and lifting up my knees. There must be lots of other positions, but we haven't had a chance to discover them. We rarely get to be alone together.'

54

I was alone, working, when Vera knocked on the door. I opened it for her; my eyes wandered to her bare thighs in the miniskirt. My eyes always followed that miniskirt, to and fro. She borrowed a rouble. I hugged her hesitantly as she was leaving; later when she returned with the rouble her lipstick was smudged, perhaps from a kiss. I followed her out to the hallway. The pain in my prostate returned.

I spent the day in my room. I wrote a little at my typewriter as usual. Then I felt tired. I drank a beer. Then I got up and fried some eggs with onions. Hans ate with me. My lunch—his breakfast. He told me about some of his experiences with women: how one time two girls had knelt at his feet begging him to sleep with them, and then one of them had pleaded with him to sleep with the other because she was torn with desire. He gave in and stretched out on the bed and said, 'Take off your clothes and walk.' She stripped and walked around, then climbed on top of him. When he got up, feeling disgusted, he made her wash him, and then left. He said she had told him about how Russian women perform abortions by inserting hot *kasha*. He said he had met a student, the daughter of a minister, who had come to see him in a private car equipped with a wireless phone and said her father was a buffoon who didn't understand anything. Her parents had quickly married her off and given her a flat in Dimitrov Street, where the ruling officials lived. He told me how once he'd been sleeping when Zoya came over to wake him up; how he had stared at her indifferently as she sat on the edge of his bed, and gradually he'd started to really want her. She held out her hand to touch him as he lay looking at her, his hands behind his head. He asked her to moisten her hand with saliva. Afterwards she went to the wastebasket by the door and wiped off her hand on the edge of it. Suddenly the door opened, and Thomas the African walked in. He stuck out his hand in greeting, 'Hallo Zoya,' and she shook his hand.

55

Yerik the Kazakh said Tatiana the teacher had invited Hans to supper at 8 p.m., and asked him to bring a bottle. Hans called Tatiana and asked if he could bring a friend along. Adnan the Iraqi came by, carrying a backgammon board. He insisted we play together, saying we wouldn't see him again because in a few days he was going back to Iraq for good. Hans went out to look for alcohol at the Berezka. Then we met up in front of Tatiana's house. The Kazakh was waiting for us. The stairs smelt of urine and vomit. We passed flat doors held closed with thick leather straps. Tatiana met us, dressed up and wearing blue eyeliner; her teeth were grey like those of most Russians. She introduced us to her guests: Volodya, who was wearing a silk print shirt and bell-bottomed Charleston trousers; and his colleague Valentin, an enormous man with a moustache who was playing with a tank-like old Russian transistor radio; Luda, a plump soft-lipped woman who sat next to Volodya, stroked his soft hair, then kissed him on the forehead.

Tatiana brought the food, looking happy. We drank white wine; I noticed a hostile, superior look on Hans' face when Volodya boasted, 'Many people have told me that I look French.' Luda looked away, embarrassed. He said she was the one who had told him that. Tatiana pointed to a bottle of rum and said proudly that Hans had spent the whole day going from Berezka to Berezka looking for whisky, but he had only found wine and Russian stuff and this Cuban rum.

The next to arrive was Boris, the Komsomol secretary for the Urals. Yerik's girlfriend called to say she wouldn't be coming; she had theatre tickets. Boris put a pillow over the telephone. Whispering, I asked Hans why. 'To muffle the microphone in case they're eavesdropping. Tongues can wag at this kind of party.' I heard Boris tell Luda, 'I'm in charge of everything here.' She responded sharply, 'Not everything.' Tatiana was talking about her father. She said that every time he watched a war film, he'd say, 'It's good, but the real thing wasn't like that.' She took my arm and suggested we drink a toast to brotherhood. We linked arms and traded kisses. She moved the table aside to make room for dancing. Volodya danced with Luda, then disappeared with her into a room. When they came out half an hour later, she seemed tired or depressed. I noticed her stealing glances at Hans. He said to her, 'Come to the *obshchezhitie* with me and spend the night there.' She said she would have liked to but couldn't. Valentin refused to dance, demanding, 'It's *rock and roll* or nothing.' Boris turned out to be a fun-loving guy. He danced with Luda while I danced with Tatiana, who felt like a floppy body made of disjoined parts. She said, 'You should come over again for my birthday, I've felt at ease with you from the first minute I saw you.' I understood that this was a bridge to Hans. She said he didn't want to come to her birthday party. Hans interrupted, saying he had his professional practicum at that time. She said she could intervene to get him out of it.

Valentin asked Luda to name her favourite colour of underwear. 'Violet,' she replied. He got up and made a call, asking someone if he had any lingerie in purple. He and Boris went out to the balcony; I followed. Boris said he was getting bored after three days in Moscow and wished he could return to his wife and kid. We opened the Cuban rum after Yerik made some ice cubes. Luda made coffee, which we sipped with *morozhenoye*. Tatiana whispered to me that Luda was looking for a settled relationship. She cast a pointed glance over her shoulder and said, 'I know Hans isn't settled—he can change his mind at any moment. My *nastroyenie*, my mood, is different.' Boris cracked a joke, and I told him, 'If all the Communists were like you, things would be beautiful.' Hans agreed. I started a conversation about the differences between reality and what was written in newspapers and books. Boris said, 'Our enemies are waiting to pounce—we can't show them all our shortcomings.' I disagreed, 'Anyway they know more about you than you do about yourselves.' He said he wouldn't be able to have this kind of conversation with his colleagues in the Urals. I heard Tatiana say something about her child, and I asked her about it. 'I mean my ex-husband,' she clarified.

Valentin said, wiping his moustache with his fingers, 'I run a big dairy plant that receives all kinds of government support. We have a summer resort on the Black Sea where thousands of workers holiday every year with their families. The plant is my life. I know every inch of it. We have 5,000 employees and I know most of them by name. I take good care of everyone. I get them all the food they need. We have two farms outside Moscow, and we sell subsidized fruit and vegetables. We also have blocks of flats, a school, an orphanage, a sports club and a house of culture.' He said he needed to leave; he had to get up early. He added, laughing, 'The plant is in its humming phase.' I asked what he meant. He said the work at the plant went in three phases. In the first phase, right after payday, the workers were hung over and slow from too much vodka. In the second phase, the work finally started to hum along. Then in the third phase, towards the end of the month, the workers were rushing to fill the quota and the products would be full of defects.

Volodya and Luda left along with Valentin. Tatiana shared her annoyance. She said she had only known Luda for six weeks; she was an engineer. She had only met Volodya last week and didn't know what he did. She thought he was an ex-con; his arms were full of tattoos. I set out for home at 2 a.m., leaving Hans.

Tatiana asked me to call her the next day; she wanted us to go out with a friend of hers. I left the house and walked to the metro station, then waited for a taxi. Gorgeous summer weather. I felt completely cheerful and awake. A slightly tipsy young man and his wife joined me at the stop. A taxi arrived; the young man ran to it, opened the back door, and with extreme courtesy gestured for me to get in. The wife sat in front next to the driver. Soon the young man asked me for a cigarette. I lit it for him. The woman turned around to him, 'Why didn't you ask for permission to smoke?' We laughed.

He asked me, 'Do you know Mayakovsky?'

I nodded, 'The poet who committed suicide.'

'Today is the 80th anniversary of his birth.' He repeated a few lines of Mayakovsky's poems about the Russian language, about Lenin and about the motherland: 'You now: / read this / and envy, / I'm a citizen / of the Soviet Socialist Union!'* Then he added, 'But now everyone wants a passport with an exit visa.'

I found the *obshchezhitie* locked and banged on the door a few times. The *dezhurnaya* opened it and cursed me out. I climbed up the stairs slowly to my room. Washed my socks and went to sleep.

In the morning I was in a good mood. Ate three eggs and a piece of tomato and took a shower. Drank some tea, then some coffee. Smoked a cigarette, thinking about the day I would spend with Tatiana and her friend. I called her at eleven, but she answered in a cold voice that sounded irate. I introduced myself and asked, '*Kak dela?*' 'I'm fine,' she replied. I asked about Hans; she said he had just left, because he had a sore throat. I said I would wait for him and take care of him. She didn't say anything about our plans for meeting, so I ended the call. I went back to the room and plunged into work.

Hans came in before noon, exhausted. He collapsed into a chair and wondered why he kept doing this. 'Doing what?' I asked. He said he was disgusted with himself; Tatiana had taken him to bed, he had lain down beside her, but then started trembling and lost all desire for her.

'But you wanted her at first.'

'I don't know.' He buried his head in his hands and started to cry. I made some coffee and spoke to him about the mother figure whom we desire but also fear because she is off limits.

56

Galia stopped by. Adnan's girlfriend, looking for someone travelling to Baghdad who could carry a letter to
him. She was petite and always smiling, with a dimple
at the corner of her mouth. She was with a friend,
Natasha. Hans took a liking to the friend. I saw she was
wearing fashionable high heels. I asked her where she'd
got them. 'They're Italian, from the *rynok*,' she replied.
'From where?' She repeated, irritably, '*Na rynke*.' Hans
explained, 'She means the black market. It's not any
place in particular, but it has stuff that's hard to find—
like tomatoes, loofahs, mohair shawls, or a pair of
Japanese tyres, leather miniskirts, women's nylons.'
Galia added, 'You can also buy a carton of American
cigarettes for 20 roubles, European chocolate and old
books.'

We bustled about preparing food while Hans went
out to buy a watermelon. We cut it open and examined
its white inside before putting it to chill in cold water.
Galia said Adnan had promised to cook her an Arab
meal before he left, but hadn't. They turned down
vodka at first, then accepted. I brought out my record
player and my three Western records. Natasha clapped

her hands when she recognized the record 'Chirpy Chirpy Cheep Cheep'. Galia listened to 'Love Story' sadly. She said it reminded her of Adnan, and that she was planning to go to Iraq. 'You should forget him,' Natasha admonished her. She shook her head and said she wanted to put out a fifth glass, an empty one, because she had promised Adnan. Recently she had been to Sochi on the Black Sea. 'How was that?' asked Natasha. She said she hadn't wanted to at first, because she had promised Adnan not to go anywhere alone, but then she had changed her mind and spent ten days there.

I danced with Galia a few times. We felt happy. Natasha watched us with interest. Hans sat out the dance, looking apathetic. Galia suggested we go to the cinema. Hans whispered to me that Natasha really turned him on. He said that yesterday he had promised to see Isadora today, because he was going back to East Germany soon.

There was a knock on the door; we pretended not to hear. Shortly afterwards I looked out the window and caught a glimpse of Isadora leaving. I felt sorry for her: she had come all that way and we didn't open the door. When I told Hans, he said he'd promised to wait for her. We went down to the park, Galia and I walking in front. I asked her how she had met Adnan. 'On the bus,' she replied. He had touched her hand and introduced himself, and she had thought that he was a *Gruzin*, a Georgian.

'When was that?'

'Four months ago. No, five.' She said she was twenty-one and had been married before; she was motherless and had lived alone for two years. She saw her father from time to time, she wanted to study English for a year and then apply to the Hospitality Institute. She asked me about life in Iraq. Was it really beautiful as Adnan always said? Working in the store was boring, and they kept two sets of account books: one for showing the state and the other with the real information. 'We pretend to work, and they pretend to pay us salaries.'

I asked her how much the dollar was worth on 'the market', as Madeleine had requested.

'3 roubles.'

We put the girls in a taxi. Galia asked, 'Aren't you going to escort us home?' We ignored her. After they left, Hans said Natasha had refused to let him kiss her. But seeing him speak to Galia in a low voice, Natasha's resistance had weakened. He said he felt annoyed and wasn't ready to waste time with her—but wasn't her body amazing?

57

Hans took off for Germany and I was left alone. Hamid and Farid and most of the Syrians left, too. The *obshchezhitie* started to look like a ghost town because of the summer holiday. Some went back to their families, others to special vacation centres. I called Galia from the payphone in the *obshchezhitie* lobby. She answered in a sharp, cold voice. I said, haltingly, 'Your friend Natasha forgot her ID card here. I have it now. What should we do?'

'We'll stop by tomorrow to pick it up. How's Hans doing?'

I said he had left the country.

She said, hurriedly, 'Call me in the morning here, please, or at work later—I have to run now. Bye.'

The guard gave me a postcard from Madeleine. It had an old picture of the weeping Virgin and just one word written on it: *Please*. I climbed the stairs heavily. I ran into Dubrovsky and his wife. He was tall, aristocratically handsome, and she was short and looked more like a labourer or village woman. He had a bottle of vodka under his arm. He invited me to come drink with them, but I declined. I opened the window but left the shutters closed against the heat. I made a salad and poured a glass of wine. Read a little of Copeland's *Game of Nations*. Then washed the dishes, put on a record of the *Capriccio Italien* and stretched out on the bed.

58

We accompanied Madeleine to the airport; she was
going home. Me, Isadora and another girlfriend. She
cried as we said goodbye. Mario wasn't around: he had
gone to a holiday resort in the south. Isadora was also
returning to Brazil in a week. We rode downtown
together. She told me she had cried in the bathroom for
a week after Hans left. Madeleine had wept, too. We
went to a cinema that was showing a film by Damiano
Damiani, starring Alain Delon. We sat next to each
other, and I put my arm around the back of her seat.
After a minute, I started playing with her earlobe; she
didn't object. I kept playing with her ear while she sat
perfectly still. I felt her shaking. She leant over to me
and whispered, 'Do you remember that night we slept
in your room?' We went back to watching the film, then
afterwards I took her back to her *obshchezhitie*.

I woke up several times during the night to the
sound of a woman in Khalifa's room. A sharp, vulgar
voice. It turned out to be Dubrovsky the Aristocratic
Drunkard's wife.

I walked to the store with heavy steps to buy bread
and *slivki*, cream. A slim girl caught my eye: yellow

sweater with long slits from wrist to shoulder, short black skirt revealing sunburnt skin. On my way back, I passed Khalifa energetically running errands, carrying a mesh *setka* of empty beer bottles.

I called up Galia as agreed, but didn't reach her.

59

Now that the *obshchezhitie* was empty, they started painting the walls to get ready for the new semester. The *komendantsha* asked me if I was going away like the others. I said no. She asked me to vacate the room for painting and offered me another room across the hall that was being used for storage. It was small and windowless, with just one bed. I stumbled over a ladder in the doorway. I stood in the middle of the room and felt claustrophobic.

I left the room and walked the halls. The painters were sitting on the floor drinking vodka. I stood watching them, and one of them said, 'Don't misunderstand. We're the working class.' I caught the metro downtown and went to the Lenin Library, which holds millions of books. I advanced through the triple doors and handed my bookbag and coat to the *babushka* behind the cloak-room counter, then gave my old card to the armed guard in his glass box. I signed my name in the register and wrote down the time. At the top of the stone staircase, under the domed ceiling, was a sea of wooden cabins: card-catalogue drawers. I wrote down the books I wanted on a roll of cardboard and gave it to the proper employee, who put it into a metal tube that led to the depths of the library. I went into one of the reading rooms laid out over a worn green carpet. Then I moved to the smoking room. After waiting an hour, I received the books I had requested. I left the library and walked aimlessly. I stopped in front of the Sofia restaurant and stood in a long queue. The waiters were coming out and fishing the foreigners out of the line to bring them inside. One of them motioned me in; two Russians in front of me protested. Then another waiter called me over; I followed him. The first one caught up with us and wanted me for himself; the two nearly quarrelled. I ate a *solianka* with meat and a vegetable salad with mayonnaise. As the vodka reached my stomach, warmth spread through my whole body.

I got on the tram. I stood next to a woman by the farebox. She was in her forties, with a nice face despite its heavy paint. She was holding a small folded umbrella. I thought she must be returning frustrated from a Sunday excursion. We stepped inside. I felt her backside behind me, so I rubbed my backside against it. She pressed back.

I got off at the Almaz Cinema. An Egyptian film, *Forbidden Love*, with Madiha Yousri and Shukry Sarhan. An unbelievable crowd. The audience showed a lively interest in the problems of a fortyish woman and her emotions, awakened after long neglect. But they laughed at the silly melodramatic situations. They were still laughing when the film ended.

I came out into a calm street shaded by trees and bisected by the tramline. I took the metro, changing at Oktiabrskaya. Crowded with people returning from summer evenings outside the city. I climbed the steps of the *obshchezhitie*, which echoed with a strange silence. I opened the door of my room, turning to look around me. I stretched out on the bed and picked up an American novella, *The Saddest Summer of Samuel S.*

I dreamt that all my teeth had fallen out but I carried them around in my mouth. They were many and small; I was afraid I'd swallow some of them before reaching the doctor. He reset my teeth and they stayed fine. I felt relieved, until they started to crumble and fall out again.

60

The newspaper *Izvestia*, reporting the latest on the dissidents' trial, alleged there was a relationship between Aleksandr Solzhenitsyn and a secret newspaper publishing news of the opposition. It said the names of four foreign journalists had been mentioned at the closed trial, during which two of the defendants, a historian and an economist, had confessed to being agents of enemy groups abroad, and to publishing *The Chronicle of Current Events*, the clandestine typewritten newsletter. It said the foreign journalists, who worked for *Newsweek* and *The Associated Press*, had served as the main conduit between the defendants and 'foreign powers hostile to the Soviet Union'. It also said the physicist Sakharov had met with the accused parties at gatherings arranged by the foreign journalists.

Izvestia published an open letter from thirty-one prominent writers attacking Solzhenitsyn and Sakharov. Among the signatories were Sholokhov, author of *And Quiet Flows the Don*, Konstantin Simonov and Chengiz Aitmatov.

The next day the newspaper reported that the prosecutor had requested a reduced sentence for the defendants because they had agreed to testify for the state. In view of the sincere remorse they had shown, he was requesting a sentence of three years' imprisonment followed by three years of exile. By exile, he meant enforced residence in a remote part of the country.

61

At last they finished painting the walls and rooms on my floor. I moved back into my room. Clean and delightful, notwithstanding the smell of paint. I stood admiring the edges of the forest through the open window. I worked on the newspapers and did some laundry. I went out to the post office. Beautiful weather, warm. The exciting smell of fresh air. My whole body was excited. I called up Galia. The line was busy. I tried again and she answered. I introduced myself again.

'I can hardly hear you,' she said.

'I want to talk to Natasha.'

'She's not here—can I give her a message?'

'Just that I have her ID, I want to give it back to her—she promised to come pick it up but never did.'

'Maybe she doesn't need it. Is Hans back?'

'He might be back at the end of the month.'

'OK, we'll visit you then. *Do svidania.* Goodbye.'

62

I didn't feel like doing my morning calisthenics. I took
a shower and left the building. The trolleybus took me
to Pushkin Square. I got off and walked past the gra-
cious old buildings, the gloomy Stalin-era buildings,
then the huge pastel-coloured government buildings,
pink, green or pale yellow, and the Khrushchev-era
blocks of flats. I walked by the bronze Pushkin statue,
its head bent in sorrow. The gigantic Rossiya Theatre
appeared and, across the street, the *Izvestia* headquar-
ters. The square was crowded with pedestrians, trucks
and buses. I passed a bakery window displaying a giant
plastic replica of a cake. A shoe store with dowdy wares
and no customers. In a fish-shop window, water poured
over a big plastic fish. Inside, only biscuits and fish in
tins; no queue. Yet the women were moving from one
shop to another, carrying their mesh bags, all eyes and
ears, alert to any little sign from a saleswoman or deliv-
ery truck that might signal that something had arrived:
fresh fish, sausages or chicken.

I went into a record store. Here I had bought
Tchaikovsky's *Serenada* and *Capriccio Italien*. They had
some wonderful organ music playing in the store and

I bought the record—a new recording of a Handel aria, *The Swan* by Saint-Saëns, a Shostakovich romance and some Kreisler, and on the B-side a Bach toccata and fugue. I also bought the Vysotsky album *He Didn't Come Home from Battle*. I felt a woman pressing against me from behind. She moved her legs so that one of them was around my buttock. I glanced at her out of the corner of my eye and found a pleasant face, a woman in her fifties. I finished making my purchase and then looked around for her—she was gone.

63

Hans came back at the start of the semester. He brought along a bottle of whisky, Western chocolate and an American *Playboy* magazine with pictures of the Egyptian pharaohs. I went with him to the Institute. He told me about the death of the socialist leader Walter Ulbricht, who had been the general secretary of the Party in East Germany: the Germans' reaction was icy. I noticed a slim girl with soft lips and a pimply but sensual face. She smiled at Hans; he spoke to her and introduced us. A Hungarian named Judit. She remarked on my broken Russian, saying it would improve quickly. She gave us the address of the house in the Taganka neighbourhood where she lived with some schoolmates.

We caught a glimpse of Zoya with one of her friends; Hans disappeared. I saw Vladimir approach her. She gave him a cold handshake. But he started talking. A moment later she saw me. I opened my arms. Hugging her, I said I had missed her very much. She said she would stop by, then walked away. Her face was plump in the traditional style of Russian women. It had lost its old magic. Vladimir followed her, and they left the Institute together.

64

I was struck again by Thornton Wilder's words: '[T]his love—of which poets make so fine a show—is nothing but the desire to be loved and the necessity in the wastes of life to be the fixed center of another's attention.'*

65

I bought 2 kilos of green peppers and put them in a glass jar with water and salt. Hans and I agreed that I would go to Judit's place to invite her over. The weather was still a little warm after sunset. I found her house. When I got closer I noticed three people: a tall young man and two girls, one of whom was Judit. She recognized me in the dark. I stopped and we shook hands. 'I'm here to see you,' I said. She introduced me to her friend, and I shook her hand. Judit asked, 'How's the Russian coming along?' I didn't answer. I held out my hand to shake hers goodbye, saying I would drop by and see her again. She said, 'We're always at home in the evenings.' She didn't shake my hand at first; then she did. I left and went on my way. Then I realized that I didn't know where I was going. I crossed the street and stood waiting for the bus for a long time along with a girl who had just stepped out of a hairdresser's shop with her hair done and covered up. I got on the trolley-bus, which took me on a long route. A tipsy young man got on and stood wobbling near the door. I got off at the end of the line, took a taxi to the *obshchezhitie* and found Hans in the kitchen. He asked me how it had gone. I said I was no good for anything.

66

In the metro I stood next to a tall woman with a prominent behind. I rubbed against her for a long time. Feeling
disgusted, I went up the escalator. Fruit vendors had
appeared around the metro station. I bought half a kilo
of apricots, half a kilo of pears and a kilo of grapes. I
looked for tomatoes; there were none. The bus was
almost empty. A forty-something lady with wide dark
eyes and full lips that had done plenty of kissing,
judging by her age. Her features looked Spanish, but
she was Russian and her body was not well put
together. She was wearing fashionable shoes with big
wooden heels and kept looking at them in wonder. I
stopped by the store in search of tomatoes, butter and
bread. No luck. There was a Russian peasant woman
on the sidewalk selling gorgeous bundles of red
radishes. I bought some. I found Hans stretched out on
the bed in his outdoor clothes. He had just had breakfast. I sat on my bed pretending to be cheerful. I poured
a glass of wine. He said he was going to see Tatiana.

There was a knock on the door, and I heard Zoya:
'Can I come in, guys?' She greeted me and took off her
trench coat. She sat down, saying cheerfully, 'I'm drunk
today!'

'How?' Hans asked.

'Upstairs. I was visiting this girl and they brought some bottles of wine.'

I asked her about Vladimir. She said, 'I bored him.'

Hans started to make a sarcastic comment. I said to him sharply, 'Do you expect this girl who's in love with you to put up with you ignoring her? Should she just keep worshipping you until you deign to pay her some attention?'

She said, 'Indeed.'

I stood up and put my hand on her head, saying, 'I'm the only one who loves you.'

She said, 'I know. I want a drink.' I poured her half a glass. She got up and came over to sit next to me. I brought my cheek to hers. Hans was sitting across from us. I was waiting for him to go out as he had announced and leave us together. I asked her if she had eaten. She said yes. I pulled her towards me and kissed her cheek; she gave me her lips, with an absent expression in her eyes and an angelic smile. She was tipsy. I took out a few records including 'The Last Waltz', to which we had danced several times before. I moved all around the room waiting for him to leave. I turned over the record and the first song came on. Hans finally left when the fast number started playing. We stood up and danced far apart; she moved with difficulty. I pulled her to my chest, cheek to cheek. The dreamy third song came on; I kissed her on the mouth. Delicate lips. Her breath was sweet. I rained little kisses on her until she opened her lips under my mouth. Her eyes were closed tight. I moved my tongue inside her mouth. I pressed against her as we moved to the rhythm of the music; she pressed back. I drew her towards the bed. She mumbled, '*Nyet*.' But did not resist. She said, 'A cigarette?' I lit one for her and we sat side by side.

'You love Hans,' I said.

'I don't know, but I do care for him.'

I took away the cigarette and started kissing her. She said, 'A drink?'

'I don't want you drunk.'

I poured her a little bit of wine. I told her I loved her and had always wanted her. She said she cared for me. I kissed her ear. She laughed delicately and her face contracted in a childlike smile. 'That tickles.'

We stretched out on the bed; our tongues intertwined. I felt incredible pleasure from her kisses, the touch of her cheek and her hair. She closed her eyes. I started feeling her clothes and tried to take off her skirt; she refused. I put my hand between her legs. Her stockings ended just at the bottom of her thighs. I rubbed there gently and she opened her legs. I tried to take off her blouse, which she refused; instead I opened a button and took out a small, long-nippled breast. I sucked on it and she began to tremble and sigh. She wasn't wet. I tried again to take off her underclothes. She refused and stood up, mumbling something I didn't hear. I went back to enjoying the feeling of her cheek rubbing mine. Then the feeling of light kisses on her lips, until heat crept into them, then moisture, and they opened to take my lips in. I pulled her to me and we stood dancing slowly. I pressed my body against hers and she stooped slightly to be at my level, pressing against me hard with her eyes closed.

I asked her if she was hungry and she said she hadn't eaten in two days. I buried myself in making food. She went up to the girls' floor to wash. She came back and sat on the windowsill, tucked a lock of hair behind her ear and asked, 'Do you remember when we went to hear Mozart together and drank beer, and how I didn't enjoy the first half of the concert?'

'This summer was bad for me—I was alone all the time.'

She said I was the only one who was glad to see her when she got out of the hospital. Then she suddenly burst into tears, saying that everyone made fun of her. I left her at that moment, hurrying to the kitchen to cut up some tomatoes for the cold cuts. I took charge of feeding her, and she cheered up immediately. We finished the bottle of wine. There was a knock on the door and Hans appeared. He said he had changed his mind and skipped his date after all. Her face lightened, and she said, jokingly, 'Wait, I need to get my clothes on.' The conversation turned to a couple in their fifties who had just got married: the way the woman had dolled herself up and everyone had surrounded her in jubilation. She wanted to say that people were mean. Hans responded, spitefully, 'Well of course—a ridiculous woman.' Zoya said she disliked people who made fun of others, liars and hypocrites. And people who run after money while paying lip service to socialism. Hans started arguing with her while I tried to mollify them. He left the room; she calmed down, stood up and put on a record, then walked over to the door, where she leant her head on the wardrobe and cried. I came over and hugged her soothingly. She said, 'I want to go. Give me my jacket.' I said no. She kept crying, repeating that everyone was against her, everyone had betrayed her, everyone made fun of her—they all thought she was insane because she had been in the hospital. The Institute's administration had promised she could return to her studies after she got out of the hospital, but her cohort was trying to stop her. She sobbed, 'No one wants me unless I'm happy and cheerful, and when I went to the hospital not one of my girlfriends asked about me.' Her tears gushed as she told about her father's illness and how she had visited the hospital when she was nine years old, bringing the patients flowers and newspapers and sitting and reading to them. And how her father's death had taken away her only friend. And how at that time she had a pet duck that would get excited when it saw her coming and welcome her. And how one day she had come home from school to find that her mother had stewed it. She said no one wanted her except to have sex with. I persuaded her to go back to the bed and lie down. She insisted on smoking a cigarette first. Then she asked for wine in the tone of an addict. Her face was flushed and her eyes were swollen from crying, making her face look completely different and much older. She lay down on the bed and I tucked her in. She put her head in my lap and curled up against me like a child, smiling. I rubbed her hair and gently scratched her scalp. I asked her if I should keep doing that and she nodded, eyes closed, and said with a childlike smile, '*Da.*'

She closed her eyes and slept. With her left cheek on the pillow, her hair made a soft wavy halo around her face. Suddenly she opened her eyes and said, 'Wine.'

'In half an hour.'

'Well, then a cigarette.' We smoked; after a while she fell asleep again. In her sleep she suddenly laughed. I closed the window when I felt the autumn chill. She woke up a little while later and said, 'It's been half an hour.'

'No. Five minutes—go back to sleep.'

'I had a dream in full colour.'

'Wide screen?'

'No. There was a pond and a strange man.' She fell asleep again after asking me to lie down beside her and hold her; she buried her head in my chest.

I dozed a little with her, then got up and went out into the hall. I saw Hans approaching. 'Depressing night,' he said.

'You were immature and she's drunk and loves you and feels that you've abandoned her.'

He said what drove him crazy was when she talked the same way as Vladimir, the same gestures and the same phrases showing that he was anti-system, anti-communist, anti-Party. We made some tea; Zoya woke up at the sound. We sat together drinking it. She was calm, smiling, alert. Hans started asking her about her upcoming exams and how we could help. He suggested that I take charge of English and he deal with Scientific Socialism and Political Economy. She said there were things she didn't understand and wasn't convinced of and had trouble memorizing. We said that was beyond the scope of the Institute. We agreed that she would come over for help, and she went up to her room.

67

On 11th September a military coup took place in Chile; the coup leaders took over the Presidential Palace and murdered President Allende. Hans said the coup would ignite revolution in Latin America and redouble the valour of Guevara's followers. I said they belonged to the childish Left; all Che had done was a silly adventure. Hans quoted a few lines from Yevtushenko's poem addressed to the Argentine revolutionary:

> Comandante, in trading you,
>> bidding the price ever higher,
> they sell your precious name
>> too cheaply
> With my own eyes, Comandante,
>> in Paris I saw
> your portrait, your beret with a star,
>> on modern 'hot pants'.
> Your beard, Comandante,
>> on bracelet charms, brooches
>> and saucers.
> In life you were once pure flame,
>> they turn you into smoke.

But you fell, Comandante,
in the name of justice, of
revolution—
not in order to become an ad
for the commerce of the
'left'-minded.*

68

Zoya appeared, wearing a winter jacket and sweatpants that disappeared into tall mud-stained rain boots. Her arms were full of flowers. She entered in a flurry and spoke to Hans, asking for a bottle. I gave her a milk bottle and a square bottle for the white lily stems and daisies. Hans was friendly towards her. She put the left-over flowers aside and pulled a few apples out of her bag, saying they were fresh, she had picked them herself. Then she took out a small piece of paper, unwrapping from it a piece of apple preserved in sugar. She cut the piece in half and said, 'Eat it.' Hans didn't seem eager, so I made an effort. I ate a small piece with difficulty. I took the other piece from her and bravely pushed it into my mouth, saying, 'Look!' I then put on Liszt's 'Hungarian Rhapsody'. She opened her bag and flourished a Truman Capote novel and her papers for English class. I made coffee in the kitchen. Hans went to fetch it. I hugged her, saying, 'Yesterday I was hoping you would be with me.' She said, laughing: 'And today, no?' She took off her scarf, let her hair down, and sat next to me. We got to work. Hans came back and sat down at his desk with his back to us. I kissed her hand one time. Another time, her cheek. She was mostly silent, sometimes beaming a childlike smile.

Hans went down to use the phone. Zoya took a knife and cut an apple into two identical halves. She dug out the core and put a red cherry pit into the middle and then closed up the halves again. 'For whom?' I asked. She replied, 'For anyone at all.' I said, 'Zoya?' She looked at me and laughed shyly. I pulled her close to me; quickly she picked up another apple and stuck four matches into it, then two cherry pits for the eyes. She made a hole in the top and stuck in a red flower like a cap and a small, angular nut for the nose. Hans came back, and I told her, 'It belongs on the *tum-bochka*, the nightstand, by his bed.' He shook his head no. She added a green stem above the eyes for brows and put the thing on the windowsill. Hans left the room again; she added two matchsticks between the eyes, bending their heads towards Hans' bed. I said, 'Looks like it's begging.' She laughed with embarrassment and quickly turned one of the matchstick heads to face my bed. She was smoking a cigarette. I hugged her, standing up, and pressed my cheek on hers. She closed her eyes and did not move. When I started kissing her, she did not resist. But she wasn't into it either. I heard footsteps in the hall and thought that she must be thinking, like me, that it could be Hans. Hans came in suddenly; we separated, and I engrossed myself in making tea. I asked him if he noticed any change in the apple. She said he was a *durak*, a fool, and hadn't noticed. I insisted he had. I said, 'The eyes are turned towards you.' He sat down and they started a long conversation. She reached for a page of *Pravda* and cut out the main headline, something about something that was supposed to 'enhance one's gifts'. She told him to look away, then pasted the clipping on the wall next to his bed. Then she announced. 'I'm going now. I'll be back for another lesson in three days.' She kissed me on the cheek, then leant over to him, and he kissed her on the cheek. She said, 'Look at that—he doesn't stand up to kiss me goodbye.' I asked if she needed me to walk her home. She picked up the rest of her flowers and said, 'No, I'll go up and see the girls first, then I'll go to my mom's house.'

69

Mikha proclaimed, 'I've got three girls. You guys are in charge of the place, the food and the drink.' He was short and chubby in a feminine way, with a delicate mouth and elongated cat-like eyes. We went to Abdel Hakim's flat; he was away visiting his wife in Ukraine. Mikha went off to meet the girls at the nearby metro station. Half an hour later he returned alone. He said, 'The girls didn't come.'

Hans looked at him with disdain and said, 'So, now take care of it.'

'How?'

'That's your problem.'

They stared at each other. I felt some hidden dialogue passing between them. Hans' gaze held a kind of mocking challenge. Mikha got up and left. He came back fifteen minutes later with two girls. Hans whispered to me, 'Street girls.' One of them was like a prostitute, with a hoarse voice, dyed hair and a shiny fake leather dress, with red spots on her hand. She drew in each breath deeply as though suffering from a cold. The other one was young and ordinary, named Lana. We started drinking, and Mikha cracked a few sexual jokes, acting them out with obscene movements. The first one said she wanted us to buy her a Japanese umbrella, one of the small folding ones. I noticed she was paying attention to Hans. Lana said she wanted to wash her hair. She asked if we had any hair curlers. We looked all over the flat for them. We found some on top of a metal cupboard. Hans phoned Natasha, then left to go pick her up. Lana took a long bath. I sat and smoked in the living room, feeling a desire to give in to slumber. I got up to go to the kitchen; passing by the bedroom, I noticed Mikha in there, dancing slowly with the other girl. I heard her say in her hoarse voice, 'I don't want. I don't want.' When they saw me they both pretended to be in harmony, swaying together to the music in silence, until I went past—then they started bickering again, and came out into the living room.

Hans came with Natasha and went straight into the bedroom with her; the grey-haired one shut the door on them resentfully. Then she left the flat with Mikha. Lana came out of the bathroom with her hair wrapped and no clothes on. She said, 'I want to sleep.' I lay down beside her on the couch and kissed her, then lay on top of her. I felt her legs and found her skin thick and rough, covered with hair. I asked her to take off her underpants. She said she had her period. I didn't believe her. I said, 'It doesn't matter.' I put out my hand and felt the cotton. She took off the underpants and put them under her head, and the smell of blood reached my nose. I lost my desire and gave in to sleep.

In the morning I found that the blood had left some marks on the couch. She asked me for a rag and some soap, saying, 'Don't be afraid, the blood is fresh.' She gave me her phone number. I noticed she was making a point of speaking to me slowly so I would understand. As though she had experience with foreigners. We had breakfast; she said no to coffee, because the doctor had warned her away from hot things. She got ready to leave and asked, 'Aren't you going to walk me?' I said, 'The metro is right there.' She snapped, '*Ladno*,' and left.

Soon Hans thrust himself into the living room. He said Natasha had left early. He said she had resisted him until seven in the morning, then given in, but he hadn't enjoyed it with her. He added that mostly when he slept with a girl he was drunk and didn't remember what was happening or even if anything happened at all. We went to the *obshchezhitie* and slept for a few hours. After dark Mikha came, drunk. He said, peering into our faces, 'Are you angry at me?' We didn't answer. He said he was afraid he might have caught something from the girl—she had been scratching at her thigh and her back the whole time; he said he had another one who's prettier. He added that he had lost his parents when he was two and grown up in an orphanage, where life had been cruel, and that he was an atheist because if there was a god he wouldn't have permitted such things. He asked about the people who owned the flat and did they need anything from abroad. And could we please look around for some jeans to buy for him.

70

I was downstairs doing my laundry; when I got back to the room I found Zoya sitting on Hans' bed wearing her coat and a hat, and holding a notebook. I asked her without preamble, 'Why didn't you come like you promised?' She said, 'My sister was in town, and that day I gave a presentation at the Institute about my *praktika,* the practical training trip. It went on for four hours, and they praised me a lot—I had written out the beginning but just talked them through the rest.' She paused a moment, then said, 'I'm a little drunk.' She added, 'This morning the doctor came by my mother's house on his rounds to check on me, and he peered into my eyes and told me to walk a few steps in front of him. He said I should return to the hospital, but I told him I had exams this month, and when he left, the neighbour invited me over for some vodka.' She said she hadn't come to study but to use the phone; she would arrange another day to come.

I pressed my cheek to hers; she closed her eyes. I touched her mouth with mine; it was dry. She told some long story about her niece and her apples. She said, 'Today's my anniversary, it's been three years—isn't that enough?'

'I think you'll leave him.'

'So do I. I'll go now.' She stopped.

'*Do svidania,*' I told her.

She stood still; I hugged her. She peeled away from me and left.

71

Lotfi arrived from Egypt. A PhD student, overweight, perpetually irate-looking. They gave him a single room on the first floor. When he heard that I lived with a roommate and before that with three, he said to me, 'You have to come to the Soviets with a lot of demands, then they'll give you exactly what you want.' I asked him about the situation in Egypt. He said, 'It's pathetic. The only thing young people care about is karate. Everyone's suffering from high prices, chaos and dog-eat-dog competition. There's a proposal before Parliament to sell off publicly held companies to shareholders, and that would mean the end of everything. When I return to Egypt in the end I'll start a company; the private sector is the only thing going now.' He said the new cultural attaché to the Egyptian embassy had bought a Volvo from Finland; he had been a member of the secret vanguard organization of the Socialist Union that Nasser had founded in his final years, then became one of Sadat's men and got sent to Moscow to take charge of the Egyptian students.

Lotfi lent me Tawfiq al-Hakim's book *The Return of Consciousness*. Some sentences were underlined:

Perhaps as they said it was his personal magic when he spoke to the masses, or perhaps it was the dream in which we had begun to live because of those hopes and promises. Whatever the fact, those glowing images of the accomplishments of the revolution made out of us instruments of the broad propaganda apparatus with its drums, its horns, its odes, its songs and its films. We saw ourselves as a major industrial state, a leader of the world in industrial reform, and the strongest striking force in the Middle East.*

72

I prepared boiled potatoes, cold meat and a salad without tomatoes. I lit the electric heater and the desk lamp. I turned off the overhead light. When I put the vodka bottle on the table along with some brine from a jar of pickled peppers, Zoya came to life. She mentioned our previous conversation and said she would stay with her husband forever because she was indebted to him; the sex with him was ordinary, nothing special, but sometimes she enjoyed it a lot; if she never reached orgasm, that wasn't the most important thing. She looked at Hans and said, 'If you'd asked me to marry you, I would definitely say no—having my husband there gives a structure to my life, because I'm a weakling otherwise.' She said she didn't mind sleeping with whomever she was attracted to, and she had introduced Hans to her husband in order to be able to talk about him freely. I said, 'Marital infidelity might be the most refined type of love, and the most innocent. It's sex solely motivated by pleasure, without—in most cases—any economic considerations.'

Talia joined us. Zoya said, 'We're having a candour session.' Talia, after two drinks, said she was generally frigid and hadn't felt sexual ecstasy until four years ago. She moved on from one love only to fall into another. She always dreamt that she was sleeping with other women. She talked about her aloof relationship with her mother; it was her grandma who had raised her.

Hans pointed to the vodka, the electric heater, Zoya, the tidy room and the desk lamp, and said, 'We'll never have another moment like this. We'll always remember it.'

Talia went up to her room. Hans invited Zoya to stay over until morning, saying, 'We have another room on the same floor that's empty.' She said no; her mom was expecting her and she had to get back so it wouldn't look like she was spending the night out. But she did not leave. I got ready for bed and wrapped myself tight in the blanket. The cigarette smell and voices bothered me. Between sleep and waking I felt him take her behind the wooden wardrobe; then, stillness. I heard the wardrobe door opening. Was he getting the key to the other room, the one our floormate had left for us while he was abroad? I fell asleep. I woke up to the sound of the door closing. The heater was on. I woke up again. Dawn light. The doorknob turned and Hans came in. I thought I heard him returning the key to the wardrobe.

73

Hans phoned Galia. She said she couldn't come see us; she had Natasha over. She invited us to join them instead. We took a taxi. It was snowing for the first time. We sat in a small room around a heaping table: bottles of champagne, watermelon, grapes and pears. A young man in a wide necktie, a red shirt and a jacket that was tight around the shoulders. A girl with Asian features named Masha, and a Yugoslav guy in jeans. Another guy introduced himself as a Jew from abroad. I heard the Yugoslav say he didn't like the Beatles but preferred James Brown. I said I didn't know him. Natasha said, 'I do!' She ignored Hans. The phone rang repeatedly, and we heard her list prices of some foreign clothes. It seemed she was brokering for someone selling or buying. When she saw me staring at her, she said, 'Well, why do you think none of us is wearing a Soviet suit or a Soviet shirt? Because every new style has to get approved at ten different levels, so it takes five years to reach us. In Khrushchev's time the police used to arrest people wearing jeans.' Galia asked if we had heard from Adnan and whether he had sent her anything. Masha leant her head on the stomach of the Yugoslav guy as he stood next to her, wrapped her arms around his waist and closed her eyes. He sat down, saying, 'We should practice onanism.' He turned to Hans and touched his face, proclaiming, 'We have no need of women.' Another guy came in, staggering drunk. They said he was Boris, the painter. He said, helping himself to a glass of champagne, 'I have no hope of being a good artist. All I can do is paint what the official organs want … You know there's a Georgian film where a character asks his co-worker, "But how do you live? In your factory there's nothing to steal except pressurized air."'

The door of a bedroom burst open on a bare-chested guy. He said our noise was keeping him awake. And that he'd go to the police if we didn't cut it out or leave. Galia said he was one of her flatmates and that we'd better leave. The Yugoslav guy hugged Hans and kissed him, saying, 'Come with me, sleep with me tonight.' Hans got rid of him. Natasha refused to come along with us. We hailed a taxi to the *obshchezhitie*. On the way Hans asked me, 'What makes a man like that?'

'What do you mean?'

'Homosexual.'

I said lots of factors—childhood experiences, the body's hormonal makeup, other stuff.

As soon as we were upstairs he threw up in the bathroom, muttering in irritation, 'She's not even pretty. She's not worth a damn, and I'm not going to care about her.' I gathered he meant Natasha.

74

I opened the door to see why it was so loud in the hall. It turned out that Belmajid the Algerian had thrown a party and invited the new female students. He was small and sprightly. I had noticed him coming and going with two or three girls trailing along. Hans joined me and we stood looking at the hallway which emptied out suddenly, then crowded again with people taking a break from the noisy dance music or just catching a breath of air. A tipsy girl came out and walked towards the end of the hall. One of the students called her; she paused. He asked, 'Where to?' She moved her shoulders theatrically to left and right, saying, 'To the toilet.' Then the Bulgarian's girlfriend appeared with her tiny doll-like face, her short dress showing her fat legs and extremely small chest. She was followed by a spectacular girl in a tight blue blouse and grey trousers, with a lovely round face, shining honey-coloured eyes, cheeks flushed with fast-running blood, short black hair and a leisurely stride indifferent to anyone who felt her magic. I had always seen her surrounded by guys. I said to Hans, 'I dare you to get her.' Anar, the Kazakh woman, came up to us with her gorgeous bust and red, always moist lips. I heard her tell her friend, pointing to Hans, 'This one is the most handsome guy here.' She asked him to translate a text from German. He invited her in; she said no. She promised to come back in ten minutes but then didn't. Belmajid brought us a copy of the *Herald Tribune*, the American newspaper, pointing to a notice from the Middle East correspondent across the breast of the front page. It said Sadat was considering a suicidal gamble to save himself and his regime; negotiations were going on between the Arabs and Israel for a reconciliation, but the Arabs were insisting they needed the show of a victory to convince their peoples to accept it.

75

Strong sunlight shone through the window. I convinced Hans to go out. We didn't need coats. Warm weather with a little nibble of cold, a fresh breeze. We walked in the sun. Sun. Sun. Calm and lovely. All of Moscow was out enjoying the sun. We walked through the gardens on the way to the Exhibition.

In front of a kiosk that was part of a large store, a girl smiled at Hans. He invited her to join us, and her friend too. Tall, with beautiful legs. A little shortsighted. Wearing a wedding ring. After talking to her friend she said she had no problem in principle, but today she had plans with her husband. She suggested we meet tomorrow afternoon. After a little while the husband came. A handsome guy. We said goodbye to them and went on our way.

At two o'clock we reached a yellow forest. The leaves were yellow or nearly yellow but not dry or withered. The sun penetrated them, lighting them up so they shone. Around it, experimental forests that had retained their dark needles. We sat on an iron bench. A woman sat nearby, staring with amazement at her legs and knees stretched out to the sun. Hans talked in a calm voice about Fellini's films. We got up and continued our walk. We reached a little lake with a few boats, framed by elegant decorations. He said every republic had a special corner in the Exhibition and this corner must represent one of the Baltic states—only they had elegance like this.

We kept walking amid the total stillness; the military music had disappeared. We were surrounded by trees in colours ranging from crimson to pink, yellow and green. On the surface of the pond the slow-moving boats spread out in various directions. The whole scene had the magic of the old paintings embedded in my childhood or adolescent memory, paintings of Europe or happiness. Happiness lasting only a few minutes. Everything still, calm, quiet, beautiful, clean and warm, with no crowds or smoke or noise or dust or vodka or cigarettes, no chatter and no cold or heat or filth.

I joined a long queue in front of a vendor grilling kebabs. Hans stood in another long queue at a beer kiosk. I heard a woman sneer at the primitiveness of the operation and a man reply to her, 'Everything in our country is like that.' Behind me stood a woman with a pretty face and fingertips marked by manual labour or kitchen work. Her companion was saying that on 1st May he had been—She cut him off, 'With whom?' He said, 'With friends from work.' She teased him and patted him affectionately on the chest. When he tried to hug her, she stepped away. He stayed in the queue while she wandered off and sat down far from the wooden box. He bought the kebab skewers and stood looking around until he found her, then walked towards her laughing. I watched the supply of raw skewers dwindle until the last box ran out. I counted the ones on the grill, afraid that those too would run out before I arrived in front of them. Twenty skewers, six people in front of me. If everyone takes three or four skewers, I'd be left with none. Then there were four people ahead of me, then just one. He told the vendor firmly, 'Six skewers.' He gave him four, leaving two for me. A crescendo of indignant comments rose behind me.

Hans bought two cups of beer. We drank and ate, watching two Georgian girls. One tall, very thin, dark, ugly, and the other short, wheat-coloured, with the aquiline Georgian nose. They kept turning towards us. Hans suggested, 'Let's go talk to them.' I said, 'It's a Soviet *nabor*, and most likely I'll end up with the dark one, whom I don't want, and the other will want you— beauty seeks beauty.' We returned to the kiosk and bought six lacquered wooden spoons. Then we headed back to the *obshchezhitie*.

76

I stood in the queue for wine and vodka; Hans bought *kolbasa* and cheese. Suddenly I discovered tomatoes, grapes and apples. A blonde girl came up to Hans, ran her hand over his body from top to bottom, and declared that she liked him. The onlookers watched the scene. The blonde said, 'Come with us. We live nearby.' And she pointed to the girl next to her. He said, 'No, why don't you both come with me, I'm with a friend.' And he pointed to me.

We all headed to Abdel Hakim's place. The blonde was very drunk. She wore a Western-style coat made of green chamois leather with old, ordinary clothes underneath. She didn't take care of her hands. The other was wide-bodied, wearing a shirt too tight for her, with small breasts. Not as drunk as the blonde. She said she knew that Hans had infatuated the blonde. The latter kept calling him Max as she hugged and kissed him. The other one took out some reading specs and a notebook and wrote a few lines. I asked her if she wrote poetry. She asked, 'Would you like to hear a short poem?' I said, 'Go ahead.' She said, 'I slept with a professor, then I slept with a film director, then a chauffeur.

And there was no difference, for this is the land of the Soviets!' The blonde told a story about a friend of hers with a complicated name and how well he sang. I asked her what she did in life. She said she was at the Theatre Institute. The bespectacled friend said she was studying medicine. Hans winked at me to say, bullshit. The phone rang. Hans answered and I heard him say, '*Da, da,* call when you get out.' The drunk one repeated how much she was into Max, and kissed him.

'Cut that out!' her friend said to her sharply.

'Why? What business is it of yours?' asked Hans.

'It is—ask her.'

The other one said, 'It's true, but I love you.' And she kissed him.

'I'm getting out of here,' her friend said.

'Stay,' Hans asked the drunk one.

'But my friend wants me to come with her.'

The other took her by the arm and led her towards the door, telling her as though coaxing a child, 'We'll come back tomorrow—we'll find him then, come on, let's go.' They left the flat. The blonde left behind a bottle of lemon soda that had been in her purse.

I called Galia. I followed Hans' advice and told her today was my birthday and I wanted her to come over to celebrate together. She said she was in the middle of cleaning her room.

I said, 'I called on Saturday and didn't find you in.'

'I was at my sister's,' she replied, and then quickly, 'What time did you call?'

'Three.'

'I was here.'

'I called again later.'

'I was here, but maybe I'd just stepped out then—call me in half an hour.'

I called her at 8.30. I gave Hans the receiver. It sounded like she was asking him whether Adnan had sent her anything. Then she said she'd heard he had got married. Hans denied knowing anything about it. He hung up the receiver and said she would call in half an hour. And if she didn't, we should call her at 9.30. We did, and she said Natasha wasn't back yet; but if she didn't show up by ten then she would come by herself.

I called her at eleven. She said Natasha had arrived. Twenty minutes later, she called back saying they would take a taxi and come right away. Ten minutes after that, there was a knock and we hurried to open the door, and there was the girl with specs asking about her friend who had disappeared. She left and we sat in silence; Hans was reading. I got up and made coffee. Galia and Natasha came at midnight. Galia was wearing heavy make-up and a light charcoal-coloured sweater over a floral shirt that completely hid her breasts. Blue bell-bottoms. Elegance and simplicity. She wished me a happy birthday. I said I had been born precisely at this minute. She asked, 'Why didn't you say so earlier?' I brought a bottle of champagne from the fridge. I looked at Galia's hands and her chubby fingers, how they ended in soft chubby arcs under long nails. I wished I could touch the softest part, the finger pad. We drank to my health. I said I had come out of my mother's belly walking and had crossed the room before falling down. Their eyes widened in childlike surprise. Natasha told about a classmate of hers who had been dating a Yemeni student until he returned home for good. This classmate had borrowed a sweater from her, then denied having taken it, but Natasha had insisted on checking her bag and found it inside. She said that when the girl slept she would snore, then get up and eat a bit of apple and go back to sleep. The girl was lazy—never washed the dishes, barely went to class. She'd have another girl come over and tell her fortune, and she frequented psychologists and neurologists.

One in the morning. Galia announced, 'We should leave.' We escorted them home in a taxi.

77

I looked out the window at the graduated colours of nature—yellow, then dark yellow, light green, dark green and red, and grey in the background. I turned around to contemplate the piles of newspapers. I was still reading a whole month's worth of papers in a day, then resting the next day.

I got dressed and went out. I took the metro downtown. I walked down the broad Marx Prospect between Dzerzhinsky Street on one side and Sverdlov Square on the other. I reached the KGB building and noticed that the pedestrians were crossing the street to avoid passing in front of it. I walked to the corner of Gorky Street and Revolution Square. The Intourist Hotel with its ugly modern glass facade. A warm greeting from Wajdi. An Egyptian journalist ten years my senior. Stocky and bald. Full of life. He had been close to a government minister; perhaps this explained why the newspaper had appointed him Eastern Europe correspondent. Or maybe it was a connection to Egyptian intelligence. He introduced me to the interpreter assigned to accompany him. She was petite and dark and I thought she was Arab; later it became clear that she was an Armenian who had mastered our language. She was called Lina. Likeable and smart, good sense of humour. Her ears perked up when Wajdi said Sadat was organizing armed brigades to dispatch the communists and leftists in the universities, and that people were raising the slogan 'The Creed, Not Sinai', saying that defending the Islamic creed was more important than liberating the land. And more women were starting to cover their heads and their legs. He talked about Nimeiry's executions of Communists in Sudan, and how he had appointed one of his supporters in the coup, a Communist Party schismatic, ambassador to Somalia, where the other communist ambassadors had ostracized him.

She suggested in Arabic, 'Walk to the museum with us.' I declined because I had an English lesson with Zoya.

78

I went to a party held by the Egyptian students to mark the anniversary of Nasser's death. There was an old poster of a page from *Pravda* hailing him as one of the heroes of the Soviet Union and a leader of national liberation worldwide. One of the students recited a poem about Nasser and got a tepid reception. The cultural advisor said that under Egypt's cultural agreement with the USSR, the Egyptian students were exempt from courses in History of the USSR, Materialist Philosophy, Political Economy and Scientific Communism. Applause from the students. He noted that the Soviet education system was one of the best in the world. Ten years after entering, a student graduates with the secondary-school certificate; there are no 'elementary' and 'preparatory' stages, no science or humanities tracks, no athletic or agricultural or vocational or business specializations— instead, everyone gets the same diploma, and there are no private lessons, either. He warned the students that their Russian classmates were writing reports about every foreigner's behaviour, morals and leanings that were going straight up to the intelligence services.

The talk turned to cheap commodities we ought to buy to take home to Egypt: home appliances such as vacuum cleaners, sewing machines and mixers. The advisor said the cheapest things of all in Russia were food, LPs and rent.

79

'Dear Hans, I'm at Lotfi's. The war with Israel started today, 6 October, at noon'—I stuck this note on the door and went down to Lotfi's room. I found Naima, his wife, crouched over the suitcase-sized Russian-made radio set. She said the reports were unclear, and that all the Arab students she had met believed that Israel had attacked us.

I went back to our room and found a note from Zoya: it was a sketch of a girl and written under it, *Greetings*. I went down to Lotfi's again. Radio Cairo was playing military marches. An Arabic station broadcasting from someplace claimed that Egypt had initiated the hostilities. We felt stunned and feared a repeat of the 1967 tragedy. I remembered the songs people sang to Nasser at that time: 'Abu Khalid, our dear hero / We'll reach Tel Aviv tomorrow!' and the songs of Umm Kulthum and Abdel Halim Hafez. How could we have been the ones to strike first? Then we searched between 14 and 16 on the medium-wave dial for the American station Radio Liberty. We couldn't hear anything clear; they were jamming the frequencies. Then we picked up the military announcement that the canal had been successfully crossed at 2 p.m. The Bar-Lev Line had fallen—the fortifications that had cost 228 million dollars. The announcer's voice was calm and composed, unlike the hysterical announcements of 1967. Lotfi said, 'Ramadan is a generous month.' His wife added, 'We're mighty.' Hassouna the Nubian said, 'The man did it! Egypt is fighting without Soviet help, led by the anti-atheist Muslim believer president.' Hamid joined us. He was worried for Damascus which had seen air strikes. But the Syrian forces had fought off the Israeli attack and managed to liberate some territory including Jabal al-Shaykh.

80

Zoya came to the room after dark. Hans ignored her, burying himself in his papers. She chided me, 'You talk a lot.' I kissed her, and she embraced me hesitantly. She said she felt a lot of affection for me. I kissed her and sucked her tongue. We drank to the success of the liberation battle, and she said, 'In your strong hands our weapons will succeed.' She didn't stay long.

I invited Hans to come over to Lotfi's. He declined, saying his friendship with the Arab students had already caused some bad talk about him. He recalled how in his first year at the Institute he had joined an Iraqi student and his wife for Ramadan *iftar* every day, and that there was a male Syrian student who was in love with the Iraqi and always sat at his feet. He had quarrelled with Hans, and the Syrians had all taken their countryman's side. I told him I was sorry to hear that. He said, 'The Russians don't like me either—I remind them of the crimes committed by the Nazis in their country.'

81

The third day of the war: Egyptian forces advanced inside Sinai. Egypt's military spokesman announced that in three days Israel's losses totalled 80 planes and 128 tanks.

The sixth day, as reported by the UPI correspondent: Intense air and land battles. Israel underestimated the threat from Soviet missiles. America has begun loading its fighter planes with missiles to help Israel, which has already received 48 new F-4 Phantom planes while 150 American pilots have passed through the Madrid airport on their way to Israel.

The eleventh day: The Soviet Union announces for the first time that it is providing arms to Egypt and Syria to help them liberate their lands. The Arab students have become expert military analysts. If the Israelis advanced, then it was surely a tactical retreat by the Syrians so they could circle around and attack from behind. I told Hamid, 'It's just a gamble. The Arab regimes don't know how to do anything but lose.'

82

At 5 p.m. I took Zoya to the Intourist Hotel. Wajdi had given me the key to his room and agreed to be away for an hour. Her heart wasn't in it. She said Hans bored her. She asked if there was any wine. I shook my head: 'I don't want you drunk.' She said, 'You want the mind—that's hard.' Some cold attempts at kissing. I told her I wanted to take her to a flat sometime, but now we had an hour. I got up to use the bathroom and when I returned, I noticed her quickly swallowing something. A birth-control pill? Or something to lift her spirits? We stretched out on the bed. The phone rang. I didn't pick up. I tried to convince her to undress; no luck. Wajdi knocked on the door. I asked if he could give me some more time; he left. The phone rang again. We decided to leave. I accompanied her back to her mother's house on the agreement that the next day we would go to Abdel Hakim's for an English lesson.

We met in the morning at the Institute. We left together and walked in silence. I gave her Abdel Hakim's phone number, and we agreed that she would call at 4 p.m. She bought some toothpaste.

She came at five. She tried to put on a show of merriness. She said, 'Let's have some coffee and get to work.' She spread out the English notebooks. Suddenly Abdel Hakim came and said he wanted his flat back. I felt relieved. We left and went to the *obshchezhitie*. In the bus we sat next to each other in silence. She was downcast. Was she comparing her feelings towards me with what she felt for Hans? The door of Lotfi's room was open, and a number of Arab students had gathered there to listen to the news. I joined them, while she went up to the women's floor.

84

I went to a Paganini ballet with Wajdi and Lina. There was no ticket for me. I convinced them to go in anyway and stood waiting outside for a chance to buy a ticket. The elderly usher, closing the theatre door, proudly said, 'There's no black market for tickets at the Bolshoi.' I left.

In the bus I sat across from a woman holding a dog to her chest. A round, rosy face with prominent cheekbones. Big mouth, blue eyes. Her face framed by wild locks of curly hair. Her features pulled forward in a pout like a spoilt child. The dog's tiny head, looking around intelligently in all directions. Her shy-looking companion. She put her head on his shoulder and said she was tired.

85

In the morning, a layer of white covered the edges of the windows. Bits of snow fell thickly, covering the mud, wiping out the grey. The dark gloomy city transformed into a white enchantress. Happiness seized her inhabitants. Everyone smiling, running in the streets, stretching out their hands to catch the velvety bolls, laughing. The hot-water boilers in the *obshchezhitie* were turned on first, then the heating. Wajdi left late that night. Lina and I took him to the airport in an official car. The Egyptian cabin crew passed us, their luggage stuffed. One of them stopped at a medicine kiosk and bought thirty packets of Vipratox liniment. When the saleswoman looked puzzled, he said they were presents for his friends and acquaintances. I bought a pack as well. As we were returning through the empty streets, we passed by the Revolution Museum. Suddenly we saw a strange, silent procession of women, their heads covered with shawls, walking four or five abreast through the falling snow towards Red Square. The driver said they were heading to GUM to stand in line for when it opened at eight. After a while he added that there was a special section in the Smolensk Square grocery department that served important people and stars, taking their orders for fine meats, caviar, cognac and sausages over the phone, while ordinary folks queued for hours. Lina avoided commenting on this. After a moment she said that winter shoes were sold for 180 roubles. She added that her birthday was coming up next month. I asked, 'Am I invited to come over and feast on *dolma*?' She said, 'Just for that? I thought to see me.' She said she had once wanted to become a lion tamer. I teased her, 'But you decided to focus on men instead?' She said she had refused marriage several times. I thought that life with someone like her could be really exciting. I liked her eyes when she smiled: full of humour, mischief, intelligence and joy. I noted her phone number. She dropped me off close to the diplomatic quarter. I sensed that she lived with an Arab man.

At the entrance of the *obshchezhitie*, I ran into Lotfi; he was smoking. He said there were some ambiguous reports about the Israelis crossing the canal.

86

Talia organized a dance in her room. Belmajid was the star of the evening. He danced with a Tajik girl, throwing himself into the dance and enjoying all the attention as everyone else stood around in a circle and clapped along. Then he danced with his girlfriend, a bronze-skinned girl with beautiful honey-coloured eyes and full lips. A Russian student came along with a tall girl in a miniskirt (symmetrical legs) and a short-sleeved black blouse (medium-sized bust). She slow-danced with him, resting her head on his shoulder, looking around the room languidly. Then she sat down beside him and waited for the next dance. Suddenly Belmajid popped up in front of her asking for a dance, just as the Russian held out his hand to start dancing with her again. The Russian looked resentful; the girl beamed. She danced with Belmajid and they chatted happily. The Russian watched them, scowling.

Anastasia joined us. Tall, big, with an attractive wide dark-skinned face and a shy smile. She was dressed up and had braided her thick hair. She asked me about Hans. I sat down next to Anar. She too asked me about Hans: 'Is he coming?' I asked her in turn, 'Are you going to wait for him?' She said, 'I will.' I examined her cleavage, her golden face, her crimson lips and narrow eyes. They played some lively Kazakh music. She protested, 'I don't want to dance to this—it's my music, and I'm sick of it. I feel so old—there's nothing I want to do any more.' I asked how old she was. 'Twenty-one,' she replied. I burst out laughing. We danced together. She tried to give me confidence in my dancing, and I in turn energetically gave in to the rhythm. She left me and went to dance with a dishevelled guy who was a good dancer.

Every fifteen minutes, the corridor blonde would appear, the one who had said she was going to the toilet. She would come in, all excited, look around with a drunken unsteady gaze, and throw herself into someone's arms to dance with him. Then they would disappear for a while and return, the guy looking around with a victorious smile.

87

Mikha came to our room; he felt we greeted him coldly and went off only to return with a Czech student named Svetlana, claiming to her that it was his room and that we wanted to meet her. She was very tall, slim, with an angelic face and blonde hair. I guessed she was twenty. We came alive. He monopolized the conversation for a long time, sharing personal information about our fellow students and professors. He told her I was from the country of Omar Sharif, and she said, 'I thought he was Lebanese—one of the Lebanese students told me so.' Mikha left when we asked him to shut up; then we made coffee and opened a bottle of vermouth, enjoying the drink while talking quietly. She said that since the Soviet invasion there had been no art or literature in Czechoslovakia. I told her about the time I had visited Prague and left with an impression of claustrophobia. She asked about the situation of our women. And complained that it was taking her a long time to get used to the Soviet Union. The food, the rudeness, the lack of elegance. We made some food and opened a bottle of vodka which we drank with the brine from a jar of pickled green peppers. Talia danced in, announcing that her new boyfriend was coming to join her now. She asked me to sign him in, so I went down to the ground floor. I didn't come across the alleged boyfriend. I phoned Abdel Hakim to check in. He said he was nervous that Egypt would sign a ceasefire agreement. When I returned, Svetlana was gone.

88

Oil ministers of the Arab countries decided to cut production by 5 per cent a month until Israel withdrew
from the lands it had occupied in 1967. World oil prices
surged.

Gloom reigned after Sadat announced a ceasefire
between Egypt and Israel after 17 days of fierce fighting.
The gleam of victory went out. In Lotfi's room there
were heated discussions about what it all meant. Some
thought it was a victory for Israel and a sign of Sadat's
rapprochement with the West.

Hans came back at ten thirty. He said he had been
at Anastasia's. She told him that she had been waiting
for him for two years.

89

As I was leaving Russian-language class, I ran into Svetlana in a miniskirt that showed her fantastic legs. I chatted with her a little and made a comment admiring them. She smiled shyly. I walked her to the cafeteria. I returned to the *obshchezhitie* through snow-covered streets. In the afternoon, Hans had a visitor, a heavy Azerbaijani girl. Moderately pretty. Her father was a well-known writer. Shy, full of virginal confusion. Didn't smoke, didn't drink. When we offered her a cigarette, she hesitated before accepting it, saying, 'I'm afraid some Azerbaijani might see us.' When Hans asked about her father's sexual life, she was seized with terror and hurried to deny that he had any emotional attachments at all besides her mother. He was too busy for anything like that. The talk turned to Azerbaijan and the regressive customs to which its people clung. She said, out of the blue, that she was waiting for the Great Love that would sweep her off her feet. And that her mother kept crying and saying that she had to get married this year. She took out some pencils and started to sketch. She drew a portrait of me looking sad. Then she drew Hans smiling and exuberant, and wrote on the bottom of the picture that she hoped he would always stay the way he was. Then she said, 'I first wanted to draw you four years ago, before you grew a moustache, but you were four years my senior at the Institute—but anyway, better late than never.'

90

Sharif returned from Syria. He described the masses crowding the streets each time a Soviet missile downed an Israeli plane. And that workers and government employees were going through a terrible inflation while businessmen raked in the profits. He left us his room key and went to stay with his Russian girlfriend. He told us gaily about how he had wanted to sleep with an Asian girl. He said, 'She pushed me away and asked if I was going to marry her. I was so turned on that I just kept repeating as I undressed, "I'll marry! I'll marry!"'

91

The Institute organized a concert to celebrate the anniversary of the October Revolution, observed on 7 November. A boring piano-and-violin concerto, sparsely attended by students. A harpist in a classic white dress. With her thin body and pale face she looked like a mummy raised from the grave. She played three encore pieces in response to applause. For her last piece she chose something called 'Farewell to Life!' I felt like she was going to go kill herself on the spot. For this occasion I had read a book about the Bolshevik revolution, *Ten Days that Shook the World* by the American author John Reed. The complete chaos that had gripped Russia after the fall of the Tsars: the spread of right-wing parties and organizations, some people's belief that socialist revolution was impossible in Russia, the theory that revolution could not be achieved in one country until the proletariat had come to power in the major European states, and how Lenin settled the matter with his slogan: 'Peace and Land.'

92

I expected the room to be empty. I was just getting ready to pull the key out of my pocket, wondering where Hans was. But when I pushed on the door with my shoulder just in case, it opened. He was sitting on the bed facing the door, and on the armchair across from him I spotted the bare legs of a woman: Svetlana.

Only the desk lamp lit the room. From the record player came dance music. On the table was a bottle of wine. Svetlana was holding a lit cigarette in her hand above her bare knees. She asked me, 'Didn't you go anywhere for the holiday?' I said, putting my net bag of food down on the floor and removing my overcoat, 'Not at all.' I put the coat away in the wardrobe and my hat on top of it. Then I took off my wool sweater and went to the bathroom to wash my face and comb my hair. I came back and drank a glass of wine and sat down on my bed, a small wooden table separating me from her. The light between us was weak, and the table hid her legs. All I could see was her face and her blonde hair gathered in a bun.

Hans left the room, and I said to her, 'What a beautiful surprise to see you today without the trousers.' She said bashfully that she had recalled my comments about her legs when she was getting dressed. She looked down at her legs, saying she didn't feel comfortable that everyone stared at them whereas it was a normal thing in her country. I said, 'The problem, simply, is that your legs are straight and well-proportioned, whereas Russian women's legs are crooked and short.' I got up and picked out one of the West German dance records and put it on. The album cover was a photo of a girl in a short dress who had exposed her breast and was holding the nipple between her fingers, staring at the camera. I told her that her legs gave me just one idea: to kiss them.

'What?'

'To kiss them,' I repeated.

She laughed, embarrassed. I showed her the album cover and said, 'Here's a pair of legs, but they're not as beautiful as yours.' She took her hand off her knees to reach for the album cover, revealing her legs in all their splendour. The light reflected off the pale golden hair covering them. I asked her if we could dance. We danced, apart from each other. She moved the lamp to the side so the light wouldn't fall on her legs, and I laughed and said her lips attracted me too. She said, 'You'll have to make do with looking at them.' She slouched down to my height. She said the fashion now was for a man to go around with a taller woman.

Hans came in while we were dancing. 'Uh . . . uh,' he said.

'So, I'll leave now,' I said, laughing.

She laughed, too, and sat down, 'No, that's enough.'

We finished off the bottle. He told me in English that he was afraid Anastasia would show up. I said it didn't matter.

I brought a bottle of vodka and a glass of pepper brine. I sat down to her left on the bed and Hans on her right. She said, 'Let's do an experiment. Each of you clear your head of any prior thought, and imagine a road, and yourself walking down it. Suddenly you see a vessel. What do you feel? And what do you do with it?' Hans said, 'I lift up the vessel and drink from it and keep walking. It starts to rain but I don't care, I feel the beauty.' She explained, 'It's the road of your life, and you meet a beautiful woman and you like her and take her with you, you drink and keep going, get it? And you?' I replied, 'Two fantastic legs, I travel up them with my lips, approaching the summit like a cat with a saucer of milk, it smells beautiful and tastes delicious and I feel wonderful.'

We were kneeling on the floor facing her legs and singing her praises while she sat there with a straight face. Hans whispered to me in English that I should take the key to the empty room and sleep there.

I went to the other room. I sat there on the edge of the bed not knowing what to do. I was not aroused, just annoyed. I found an Arabic book on the adventures of Casanova, read a little and tossed it aside. An hour passed. I lay down and went to sleep. I woke up several times during the night.

In the morning, Hans said, 'I danced with her and she pressed her stomach to me. But kept resisting. I sat on the floor at her feet and kissed her legs and played with the hair on them, and she was just about to give in when all of a sudden she said she didn't want to and would hate me if I kept going—yet it didn't occur to her to get up and leave.'

93

Hans took a bottle of vodka up to Anastasia and her Italian roommate Emilia. I followed him and met Zoya on the stairs. She asked, disturbed to the verge of tears, 'Is he with Anastasia now?' She left me and continued up the stairs. Later we came down to our room and finished the bottle. Anastasia brought two more. I danced with Emilia, who said she had posed nude for some pictures in her room. She was slim, with dark rings around her eyes. She said that in the West there were more cars but also more crime, unemployment, inflation, illiteracy and plain hostility—no one was safe in the streets.

She didn't stay with us long. Anastasia fell asleep with Hans on the floor and I on my bed.

94

I was struck by a passage in the novel *The Volcanoes Above Us* by the English novelist Norman Lewis:

> What she suffered from was an almost unhealthy craving to be loved all the time. It was not merely sexual intercourse she wanted. She couldn't tolerate the benevolent decline into which even the most fevered of loves must eventually settle.*

Late in the morning, I went to the Institute. In the lobby I noticed an olive-skinned woman. My heart beat faster when I realized she was Egyptian. Over thirty, full-bodied, wearing a black jacket and slacks with a belt from which dangled golden medallions. Eyes heavily ringed with green kohl. I walked up to her slowly. I heard her tell one of the students, 'In Egypt I don't get a lot of exercise... The car is right in front of the house.' She seemed relieved at the success of her car ownership announcement. I walked away immediately.

95

Dinka, an Uzbek student, invited us to her birthday party. As we were getting ready to go up, Zoya came in. Hans left, carrying a bottle of champagne. She said she wanted to drink vodka. We put on some music. I noticed her gloom and said, 'Whatever's between him and Anastasia can't compare to what he had with you.' We got up to dance. I kissed her and sucked on her lips. I asked her to take off her skirt, but she refused. 'I can't. I'll be with you, but you have to wait. I like other people to wait for me. I don't want to mislead you by sleeping with you.' Her cheek was hot, as though she had a fever. She wanted to press her stomach against me, but I stepped back. I put on my shoes, and she said, 'Now you'll go and dance.' I invited her to come with me; she refused.

I too went up carrying a bottle of champagne. Dinka's room was decorated Oriental-style. Camels and embroidered saddles, a scrapbook with pictures of minarets and saints' temples, two photos of Lenin and Charles Aznavour and a set of Russian *matrioshka* dolls. Dinka was surrounded by girlfriends: Anastasia, Valia, Larissa, Emilia the Italian, another who was ugly and extremely tall, and an amazing one, Tamara. Eastern features, full lips and a fairy-tale body in a golden blouse that clung to her chest. I danced with Dinka, then with Tamara. She moved her body and especially her rear, uttering small husky moans all the while. As though having sex. I danced with her again, and in the middle of it she said, 'Dance with that girl,' pointing to the tall one. I went up to her and asked; she said she didn't want to dance. I sat silently watching Tamara chatting with Valia stretched out on the bed. Valia's face had a strange expression. Between pain and disgust. At times she spoke delicately, her hair piled atop her head. Hans was in Anastasia's embrace on the next bed. Tamara went over and asked him for a dance. The songs were English or American; she kept singing along. She said, looking at Hans, 'This song is "I'm Waiting for My Man".' I asked Valia to dance and she arrogantly refused. A Russian guy arrived; he sat on the other bed looking at Emilia's backside encased in tight trousers. Valia left, soon followed by the tall girl. Hans said he had a piece of hashish from Kazakhstan and suggested we smoke. Dinka said no thanks; we went downstairs with Anastasia and Tamara. We smoked a number of joints. Anastasia said she was tired and was going upstairs to sleep. Tamara said she'd stay a little longer and join her. We sat on the floor. Tamara said, 'I want to fly really high. Give me some wine.' She passed out, then threw up, then stretched out on the bed. After a while Anastasia came back and took her upstairs.

96

I wanted to do some work, so I laid out the newspapers that covered the Black September massacre devised for the Palestinians by the Jordanian king. There was a knock and Anastasia entered. She said she wasn't feeling well since she had seen Hans at the Institute with the Czech girl. I said, nonchalantly, 'He's like that.' She said she knew that, but she couldn't look at the matter rationally because she was in love with him. Also she didn't understand what I was doing with all those newspapers. I replied, 'Neither do I.'

97

Hans invited me up to Anastasia and Emilia's room to finish his bit of hashish. I felt that he wanted to be alone with the two of them. But I joined him anyway. We sat on the floor listening to the music and smoking. He said, 'Some people say there are 90 different sexual positions, and others say there are only 6.' Anastasia asked, 'And what do you think?' Emilia interrupted, 'As for me, I can't recall.' Hans put his arms around Anastasia and pulled her closer. I looked at Emilia and thought it would be appropriate for me to do the same. But the coldness I felt from my prostate took away all desire. I pleaded fatigue and left them. In the hall I met Belmajid. He followed me to my room. I made us tea. I asked what his plans were after graduation. He said he didn't want to go back to Algeria and serve in the army. I asked him if things were serious with his girlfriend. He said, 'I've dated an Englishwoman, two French women, a Dane, a Finn and a German, and I wasn't happy with any of them. Perhaps I'm looking for a copy of my mother. I want a life without women, then I'll feel pure.' I said, 'That's funny. I can't imagine life without women, and it's only when I'm with one that I feel pure.'

98

I ran into the huge Anastasia in the *obshchezhitie* lobby. She gave me a piece of paper she had in her hand: a phone message from my former teacher Nadezhda saying she was in Moscow. She lived in a faraway city with her husband. We had spent some time together when she was teaching me Russian. She had left the phone number of her hotel. I called and claimed I wanted to see her right away. She said, 'It's late, I'm already getting ready for bed, I have a ton of work in the morning. I'm here with a group of colleagues for a conference.' I asked how long she would be in Moscow. She said, 'Three days.' We agreed to meet the following day. I forgot to ask her to wear the miniskirt and red stockings from last time.

The next day I showered carefully and took a little nap after lunch. I bought a 9-rouble bottle of Armenian cognac. I double-checked the dollars in my pocket in case I needed to take her out for a meal at the National. I took a taxi to the hotel. The driver asked, 'Where are you from?' I told him. He said, 'How come you guys can't hit the Israelis? And now they've got a new piece of your land.' I didn't respond, so he said, 'We helped you guys, but then you really gave us the shaft when Sadat kicked out the Russian advisors. Not like six years ago, when we took up a collection for the kids in Vietnam—those guys sent us thank-you notes.' He dropped me off in front of the hotel. I paid him 2 roubles.

I knocked on Nadezhda's door. She opened, and I gave her a big hug and kissed her. Her mouth tasted like she hadn't eaten in hours. I held her at arm's length and looked at her. She was wearing a short floral dress with buttons down the front over a pair of trousers; still slim, black hair cut to shoulder length. She helped me off with my overcoat, scarf, jacket and *shapka*. We sat next to each other. I opened the cognac; she wasn't drinking. She went to a small fridge and came back with two bottles of lemon soda, some slices of cold meat and some bread and butter. I got up and kissed her, pretending I couldn't believe she was actually here. She kissed me back, and our spectacles bumped; she took hers off and clung to me with her eyes closed, breathing deeply. She moved her tongue in my mouth with skill, and when the saliva met on our lips she stepped back and asked me to return to my armchair.

She asked me maliciously about my Brazilian girlfriend. I said she had gone home. I asked about her husband and she replied, without a pause, 'I love him and I'm happy with him because he loves me and can't imagine life without me and trusts me totally and has no idea that I would cheat on him.' I asked her ironically, 'And how are you? Are you content with your life?' She said,

'Of course, the work is reasonable and they've raised my salary and given us a new flat, and the boys are great, everything's in its place. How about you?' I didn't answer but stood up again and kissed her. The hair she had let down around her face got in my mouth and spoilt the kiss. She pushed me back towards my armchair.

'Why?' I asked. 'I want to be near you, we haven't seen each other in a long time.'

'You saw me last year.'

'Your husband was there the whole time.'

'Well, so was your girlfriend.'

I sat next to her and this time I put my hand on her thigh and asked her to take off her trousers but she said no and sent me back to my armchair. She got up to fiddle with the radio dial and I stood up, too, and embraced her. I put my hand on her breast and after a moment she moved away from me gently.

She asked, 'Why are you unhappy?'

'Because you're not with me.'

'How old are you?'

I told her.

She said, 'I'm still young.'

'Are you thirty now?'

'No.'

'Twenty-eight?'

'No. Here's my passport. I'm twenty-four.' I recalled that she had said the same thing when we were together a year earlier.

'Do you have a boyfriend?'

She met my eyes and smiled, 'I only have one, still the same one up to now—what about you?'

'I can't find someone I like. I don't care for blondes or phonies.'

'My husband also can't imagine the scent of another woman and doesn't like blondes. Listen, I only have till the day after tomorrow.'

'Spend it all with me.'

'OK.'

The phone rang. I heard her list the ballets—*The Nutcracker*, *Don Quixote*, *Giselle* and *Spartacus*—then make a date to visit the theatre the next night. I feigned anger. She said, 'I didn't know you meant the evenings too.' After a moment, she stood up and I hugged her. She said, 'I can't, I don't want to, and anyway it's late, ten thirty, you should go.' I said, 'I love you'. She started feigning sadness. I thought she was playing the role of someone in a big dilemma. I asked, 'Is there a physical issue?' She said no. I said, 'But we've slept together before.'

I recalled that miserable time when she had undressed on her own. I was shy and reached out to hold her, so she had thought I wanted to undress her and gone ahead and taken off her orange sweater. She told her husband she was attending a women's meeting, her first time doing anything like that, she said. When she stood up naked I kissed her thighs, she smelt clean, and she gave in, but without responding, as though just watching everything happen, and I was surprised to find her too wide, possibly from the births. I moved away from her and lay on my back; she climbed on top of me but awkwardly, as though confused and inexperienced, and I heard her say, 'A girl needs a bit of practice,' and then she said she had to go or she'd be late. I was bored with my prolonged erection; we got dressed.

Now she buried her face in my chest and said, 'Yes, but after that my life with my husband became difficult for a long time.' I said, 'All right, I'll leave.' I smoked a cigarette, then stood up and walked to where I had hung my overcoat. I walked slowly, watching her from the corner of my eye, expecting her to stop me; I had felt she was playacting. She looked confused. Then she got up, switched off the light next to her bed, picked up two postcards, put them in her overcoat pocket and said, 'I'll come with you.'

'Why?'

'I'll walk you home, then take a walk and mail my postcards.'

I hugged her tight and she responded, panting a little. I unbuttoned the top of her dress; she didn't resist. I bared her shoulders and kissed them, then her chest, and suddenly I thought that I really did feel like leaving. I continued unbuttoning; she stopped me, saying she didn't want to. I left her and finished putting on my overcoat. She donned hers as well. We left the hotel and walked on the ice in silence. She pointed to the metro station. She paused in front of a mailbox and threw her two cards in. At the station I told her, 'Go home now.'

'Will you call tomorrow?'

'I don't know, maybe.'

I walked down to the platform laughing ironically at myself.

In the morning I didn't feel like talking to her, but I gave her a call at nine. She said she had called me half an hour ago; she was afraid I might kill myself. She said she had felt very sad after I left the previous day and now she couldn't work. Then she asked, 'Won't I see you tonight?'

'Difficult. I'm going somewhere with a friend, and by the way, on Saturday I can't come in the morning.' (I imagined we would go out shopping together and it would be completely boring.) 'I'll come in the afternoon. *Bye bye.*'

She was silent; I hung up.

I went up to the room and found Hans with the arrogant Valia. I sat down to flip through an old issue of an American magazine. She said she wanted supper. Hans made some and we opened a bottle of vodka. She said she used to be in love with a guy who was married; then she corrected herself, 'I still am, and he loves me too.' I put my arms around her, saying, '*Ya lyublyu tebya,*

I love you.' I ran my hand over her extremely soft cheek, and my chest pressed against her big breasts. I tried to kiss her; she pulled her face away and raised her hand to her lips. It was soft and supple, and I found pleasure in kissing it and sucking her fingertips. Hans suddenly left. She asked, 'Where did he go?' I said he had gone upstairs to his girlfriend's. She got annoyed. I tried to kiss her again but she said she had to go up now.

Zoya knocked on the door shortly after she left. She seemed tipsy. She said she had had a fight with her husband and moved to the *obshchezhitie*. She refused to sit down and said, 'You remember my friend Natasha?' I nodded yes. 'She thinks my relationship with Hans is immoral because I'm married—did you know her father is a taxi driver and a Jew?' She left.

99

I got a call from Wajdi. He was in town from his new base in Helsinki and wanted to see me. Also he wanted to buy a big spoon and knife. I asked, 'You can't find those in Helsinki?'

'But that would be for currency, and here it's cheaper.'

I ate slowly, not denying myself plenty of onions, and went to Wajdi's hotel. He presented me with three pairs of disposable women's panties made out of paper. He said, 'Perhaps they'll be of use with the ladies,' and added, 'Won't you introduce me to one of the girls at the Institute?'

I took the panties and promised him I would. I left him and got on the metro to Nadezhda's hotel. I arrived at 6.45. She was waiting. She offered the remainder of the cognac and took off her specs.

'Sorry I'm late. When are you leaving?' I said.

'At eight.' I stroked her hair. She complained, 'I was alone all day, and yesterday too I wanted to see you.'

'It's your own fault.'

'I know.'

There was a pimple on her lip. I kissed her neck and began peeling off her trousers. She said, 'There's no time.' I continued removing the trousers. I kissed her thighs and ran my finger down them while kissing her breasts.

'You're hurting me,' she said. Desire wasn't exactly sweeping me away either, but I got between her legs; our position was uncomfortable.

'I have to leave,' she said, and pulled up her trousers. I carried both her bags and stood with her until she and her colleagues drove away. She said, '*Do svidania*,' and blew me a kiss.

I went back to the *obshchezhitie* and met Valia in the lobby. She was wearing a blouse that showed off her breasts and a long 'maxiskirt' with a slit in front. I took her hand and raised it grandly to my lips. We walked into the snack bar together.

'What were you planning to have?' I asked.

'An orange.'

'We have some upstairs, come.'

We went to the room. Hans wasn't there. I tried to kiss her; she pulled her face away.

She said, 'Don't be in a rush, I need to make sure first. Yesterday I didn't feel you were glad to see me.'

'Because I thought you had come for Hans.'

She said she wanted to leave. I asked, 'Would you like to go out tomorrow?'

'Why not. Stop by.'

'No, you stop by. Four o'clock.'

100

We went out together at four and walked on the accu-mulating snow. She pointed to a passing taxi but then said, 'The best is to walk to a taxi stand.' We stood there waiting. She had wrapped her head in a scarf, Russian-style. There was a crowd to get a cab, and a drunk tried to cut us in line; she pushed him, saying to the other people in the queue: 'Isn't there a man among you to stop him?' As we got in, the drunk and one of the onlookers got into an altercation.

'Restaurant or cinema?' I asked her. 'After that I'll have to stop by one of my friends for some work.'

'Cinema, then restaurant.' We got in a taxi and headed downtown. We stopped by Dom Kino.

She said, 'Why don't you get out and go see if they have tickets for us in case we have to continue the search by taxi.' I refused and insisted we send off the taxi together; she put out her hand for me to help her out of the car. It was sold out, so we went to a seafood restaurant. There was a long queue. She said, 'Let's go to the National.'

'We won't find a table because it's Sunday. And I don't have dollars on me. What do you say we buy some food and go to my friend's flat?'

She agreed; we went into a shop. She said she wanted champagne; she had tried it at our place for the first time and loved it. I bought a roast chicken and a bottle of champagne. I stood in the queue for fruits and asked her, 'Apples or pears?'

'Both.' I bought half a kilo of each.

She noticed some cucumbers and clapped her hands. I bought half a kilo of those too. We were close to Abdel Hakim's house and walked over. She left me to carry my bag, the bread, the apples, the pears, the cucumbers, the bottle of champagne and the chicken while she walked next to me with her hands in her pockets, lost in her private world. Just in front of Abdel Hakim's house the bread slipped out of my hands. She stood looking at it until I picked it up. A group of men was in the stairwell drinking vodka. We went up to Abdel Hakim's. I knocked; no one answered. I waited a while and then knocked again, in vain. Finally we left and went back to the *obshchezhitie*.

101

Wajdi asked me to look in on the daughter of a friend of ours. Faiza. A student at the Polytechnic Institute. I went to the *obshchezhitie* she lived in. I found her sharing a room with an Iraqi girl. Faiza was slim and shy, with a round white face, about twenty. Her Iraqi roommate was dark and broad-shouldered, a clearly masculine type, and looked at me with hostility.

I asked Faiza about the head of the student union, an Egyptian, and she said she had quarrelled with him because he wanted to declare films and theatre un-Islamic and at a party in memory of Taha Hussein he had accused him of atheism; he had also attacked the Soviets and said they weren't helping us.

I looked at the room and noticed that the two beds had been pushed together. I asked how she spent her free time. The Iraqi interrupted, 'We don't have any free time—the course of study is hard.' I asked Faiza, 'Don't you have a boyfriend?' She blushed and said faintly, 'No.' I continued, 'So do you ever go dancing? I could invite you sometime.' The Iraqi put her arm around her shoulders and repeated defiantly, 'We don't have the time.'

102

As we were leaving the Institute we met Nadia. The secretary of the dean for foreign students. Medium height, graceful. A supple body, full of life. I would always see her rushing around the halls. She had stopped to flirt with Hans. I said a few flattering words; she paid me no attention. She told him she was working late that day. He asked, 'Should I come keep you company?' 'Sure,' she replied in a hoarse voice.

Snow covered the ground, and the air stung. I pulled the *shapka* down over my ears and tied it under my chin. I walked gingerly, afraid to slip. We bought a bottle of Starka vodka, a bottle of vegetable juice and some *zakuski*—pickles, radishes and a bag of roasted potatoes. He said, 'Let's take a taxi.'

'That will be expensive. It's far away.'

He noticed a quasi-military jeep with a Russian guy standing next to it who looked gentle and shy. He called to him, 'Sasha, where are you headed?'

'Where do you want to go?'

'Elektrozavodskaya Station.'

'Hop in.'

The car began to move. Hans whispered to me that the guy worked as a driver at the Institute and was Nadia's boyfriend; they were getting married at the end of the year. I said to the guy, 'Maybe I've seen you. Once I opened Nadia's office door and saw her bent over a seated guy kissing him.'

He didn't respond.

When we got off by the metro station, Hans said, 'You shouldn't have told him that—it might have been someone else Nadia was kissing.'

We looked for the dormitory where Tadros lived, walking hunched over with our heads down against the cold and snow. Twice I slipped and almost fell. Finally we found the building. He welcomed us warmly. He was heavy, medium height, wide-faced, dark-skinned, about forty. He was studying for a PhD in agriculture. We walked into his clean, neat single room. I rubbed my frozen fingers and said, 'Let's have some vodka.' He opened the inner window and took out some white cheese, some fish and some Egyptian hard cheese. On the walls were photos of Russian masses carrying red flags, and next to them a piece of paper with some lines of an Egyptian patriotic song. A little statue of the Virgin stood above his bed, and there were a few icons of Jesus and the saints. Next to the bed I saw an oud. When he saw us staring at it he said, 'I've loved music since childhood, but I'm from a conservative family in Upper Egypt and my dad wanted me to have a respectable future. I became an engineer, then an assistant teacher at the university, and now I'm getting a PhD, but I still love to play.' After the first drink, he picked up the instrument. I said, 'But first, let us hear Sayed Darwish's *Scheherazade*, since you invited us over for it.' Looking peeved, he got up and put on the cassette. There was a knock and a Russian girl came in, plump and ordinary-looking. She was taken aback by the sight of us. She took off her overcoat but kept her head covered even as she sat down. She said she was going away the next day. Tadros greeted her politely and respectfully. He told me she was his classmate's wife and a fellow graduate student. She started talking to Hans. She would speak fast, then get distracted. She didn't want to drink. Tadros told me that she had met him at a gathering; seeing him sitting alone, sadly in the corner, she had joined him to cheer him up, danced with him and asked to come down to his room, where they had talked for a long time. The girl stood up and gave him two painted wooden spoons. On the wrapping paper she had written the name of the village where they were made. He tried to show her that he already had two spoons like them. She said, 'You're staying longer, but I have to go. You won't see me again for two months. Maybe I'll stop by again late tonight.' She left. He picked up the oud and played Sayed Darwish's 'Al-Hashashin'. I requested Muhammad Abdel Wahab's 'When I See You Next to Me'. He said, 'Abdel Wahab plagiarised Sayed Darwish and caused his death.' But then he played 'Cleopatra' and 'The Gondola'. Another girl came in; she was plain and pale.

She sat down and pushed the scarf covering her ears down to her shoulders. She said she had just finished gathering research materials for her dissertation at the Central Gas Organization and was now going back to her son in Khabarovsk. He told her, 'You're not happy and you know why.' She said she had just bought a flat, paying 1,500 roubles upfront and the rest in instalments. He advised, 'You need to find a man.' She looked at him bitterly. I thought she had tried with him but he either didn't get the hint or didn't want her and she had despaired of trying again. She asked him to sing a song in English and corrected his mistakes. Then he played Farid al-Atrash's 'Flower of My Imagination'. She said she had liked that melody since she was a child. He told her it was the Arab tango. She left. We finished off the bottle and got ready to leave. He announced, 'Now I'll play you my favourite piece.' He played Umm Kulthum's 'Wave After Wave'. He said: 'We can't escape this music. It's inside us, not only because it's so splendid and beautiful but also because it's so entwined with so many moments of our childhood and adolescence.' He was looking at Hans while he played, and I saw the latter put his hands over his lips as though to hide them. Every time Tadros felt we were about to get up he'd make us listen to one more piece. We agreed he'd come to our place the following week. He said, like a big performer, 'Come pick me up.' He shook my hand goodbye but kissed Hans on the mouth.

103

Sharif showed me a letter from Adnan. He wrote that he had been appointed to a government job and was facing a daily war of nerves at work. He added: 'I'm getting married soon. Tell Galia I've only received one letter from her, and give her my address.'

I tallied my purchases to split the bill with Hans: 130 kopeks' worth of eggs, 30 of milk, 364 of vodka, 80 of bread and sesame *halva,* 80 of vegetables.

Haydar the Lebanese and I got to talking about Naguib Mahfouz's book *Under the Umbrella.* Haydar sported shoulder-length hair, chewed gum and wore fashionable bell-bottoms, a blue leather jacket and red-and-blue shoes with thick heels. He said Mahfouz had wanted to accuse the USSR of seeking to occupy Egypt. He pointed out the passage in the book, and I found it more applicable to the United States. I said, 'You're just projecting your own ideas.' He didn't deny it. He said his project after he returned to Lebanon depended on seeking help from Communist Party members who would work for free! He said he wanted to exchange dollars for roubles. He also said the price on the black market was 3.40 roubles per dollar, but if we waited a week it might go up as high as 3.60.

At the Institute I ran into Nadia in the hall. She was standing in front of a window looking at herself in the glass. I noticed she was crying. I put my hand on her shoulder and asked, 'What happened?' She dried her tears and replied, 'The man I loved turned out to be involved with organized crime.'

104

This time Galia received us in her little room. We could hear her flatmate's TV from the other room. Her friend shook our hands with her fingertips. I noticed that Galia's stomach was bulging and she had tried to cover it up with a colourful shawl. Was she pregnant, and was Adnan the father? We avoided mentioning his name. She didn't put out an extra glass for him. I felt some hostility from her friend. She turned down my Indian cigarettes in favour of filtered Russian ones, saying, 'Our cigarettes.' She smelt like she hadn't bathed in days. She kept scratching her head and rubbing behind her ears and the back of her scalp. Galia was scratching her head, too. She served us some mushrooms in *smetana*, sour cream, with garlic and some homemade wine. Hans asked how she was doing and she said, 'I'm happy, we have to live our lives. Everything happens according to a plan.' She turned on the TV and we watched Brezhnev's visit to Cuba. When he returned, all the big officials of the state and party were waiting for him at the airport. The chairman of the Presidium, Podgorny, approached him. He shook his hand and turned to Prime Minister Kosygin and embraced him; the latter tipped his hat, baring his head to the falling snow, and Brezhnev gestured at him to cover it again.

When we left, Hans went off alone to Tamara's.

In the morning I looked out from under the covers and saw that Hans' bed was untouched. I imagined the full-lipped, full-bodied Tamara, everything about her shrieking femininity, making the throaty sounds she sometimes made. I heard a knock but didn't answer. Someone opened the door, looked in, and left quietly. Anastasia? I met Hans at the Institute. He was tired and his lower lip was swollen, clearly from a bite. He said he had spent the night at a Berezka. I asked, 'How's that?' He said Tamara lived in a big flat full of all kinds of foreign goods and worked as a model—no doubt she had ties to the black market.

105

I went to the clinic for an electrocardiogram. I lay down on the table, scrawny and naked to the waist. The doctor checked that I was hooked up to the device. After the ECG, she advised, 'Avoid drinking alcohol.' I left the clinic, my head bowed and body hunched against the falling snow. My fingers froze inside the leather gloves. At the clinic I had heard them talking about the weather—it was 30 below. I thought: the nearby fish restaurant only serves wine, and I wanted vodka or beer. I took a side street to Kalinin Prospect, then the underground passage across the street. I passed the gigantic Prague Restaurant and headed to a *stolovaya*. I expected a queue outside its door. There was no one. I climbed the stairs and saw a sign: 'Closed today.' I came back down. I thought of going to the end of the street, to an underground restaurant that charged a rouble to enter. I decided against it: fancy places made me nervous. I walked around the building. The ground-floor bar was also closed; people were milling around at the doorway, which displayed a sign saying it was full. I kept walking. People clustered around stores closed for the lunch break, waiting for them to reopen so they could buy New Year's presents. Onward to the Prague

Restaurant. I pushed the outside door open, expecting the uniformed doorman to stop me. But he was busy talking to someone; I took the opportunity to push the second door. I relaxed when I saw ordinary Russians checking their overcoats at the *garderop*. I took off mine and looked in the giant floor-length gold-framed mirror: the green sweater stretched out from washing, the trousers frayed at the cuffs, the shaved head, the shirt collar that had worn out some days earlier. The foyer was wide. I climbed the broad spiral staircase carpeted in red and overlooked by giant mirrors. Upstairs, spacious rooms. I headed for one of them and was stopped by an aged waiter. 'Where to, young man?'

'I want to eat.'

'Not here. Here people gather for occasions, for meetings. Go up to the fourth floor.'

I continued the climb. A circular room under a glass ceiling. Most tables were occupied. I stood at the entry. Many waiters came and went but no one paid attention to me. One carried several bottles of Narzan mineral water. The table next to me was full of foreigners from Eastern Europe. They were drinking sedately and staring at a Russian girl's backside. The head waiter, who looked like a wrestler, came over. He asked what I wanted.

'I want to eat.'

'There's no room, go stand further away, by the entrance,' he said calmly.

I sat on a chair, near a round table where an old lady was sitting. I prayed she wouldn't invite me to sit with her. An elegant waiter brought her a bottle of wine, placing it on the table. She got up and moved to a seat facing the mirror. Then she returned to the previous seat. Her hair was dyed. The waiter brought three bottles of lemon soda and arranged them on the table. She called him, 'Valia, bring me some glasses.' He brought two. She filled them with wine and rearranged the bottles. She asked him for a cut-glass fruit bowl; he brought it for her. She put it on the edge of the table, empty. She said, 'Now it will look like a full table.' He brought her the *zakuska*. A Russian came and joined me. Some of the diners started to leave. The waiter came and told us, 'You will have a table in an hour and a quarter.'

The Russian said, humbly, 'But we've been waiting here a long time.'

'It's not my problem how long you've been waiting.'

Half an hour later he let us in. We sat next to a table of three men who were dressed up Western-style, but Russians, who had a spread of vodka, caviar and tomatoes. After a while the head waiter came. Every time I ordered something he shook his head and said, 'We don't have it.' I nodded towards the next table and said, 'But you have tomatoes.'

'They ordered ahead this morning.'

He brought me a bowl of *solyanka*, a Prague salad, a broiled hen in garlic sauce and 150 grams of vodka. I watched a Georgian general with a Georgian woman devoid of beauty. When I finished my salad, my neighbour filled his glass and insisted we drink together: *Za zdorovie!*

I offered him a cigarette, and he asked, 'Where are you from?'

'From Egypt, and you?'

'I'm a Jew from Ukraine.'

After a moment, I asked, 'Do you get any trouble? I smell some anti-Semitic spirit here.'

His face took on a strange expression, something like fear. 'No. I'm a Komsomol member and an engineer —I'm leaving Moscow tonight.'

'If you were born in Ukraine, how come you don't call yourself Ukrainian?'

'My passport says my nationality is Jewish.'

'Someday, people's religion or nationality won't matter.'

He didn't comment. When we finished he hurried to pay his bill and leave, without so much as a *Do svidania.*

106

Anastasia spent the night in our room, asleep in Hans' arms on the bed across from mine. I was surprised the narrow bed could fit them both. She left at 6 a.m. He slept on. I got up at ten after enjoying an hour of strange semi-sleep. We made breakfast: toast with butter and jam. We sipped our tea to a Haydn symphony. We went out on the snow-covered street. A shy, hesitant sun. No cold wind. I didn't tie the *shapka* strings under my chin. It reminded me of the winter chill in Cairo. I inhaled with pleasure. I said I wanted to hurry and see the Truffaut film.

The film began, at the screening room on the third floor of the Institute. The stupid school, the degenerate, cruel teacher and the child groping for a path through all this, and forced to lie. At home his mother has no time for him. She gets home late, exhausted, after he has already set the table. The father comes home, a failure, and at night the child can hear them arguing. He has seen her kiss a man in the street. He runs away from home. She brings him back and decides to be nice to him, gives him a bath, and when he wants to go sleep in his bed in the living room by the door she says, 'No, in our bed.' He goes to her bed and undresses and slips in naked.

My eyes filled with tears more than once, and I saw Anastasia crying, too. We left the room together. She showed me a picture of Kosygin in the newspaper, above the fold on the front page, receiving a top medal. She whispered to me, 'They just scratch each other's backs.'

107

Abdel Hakim went away with his wife to spend the New Year holiday in her village, leaving his flat key with me. I invited Zoya to join me. She said she was too busy. I went by myself. I bought a bottle of cheap Algerian wine, half a kilo of apples, four eggs for the morning, a bottle of milk, a bit of fish and two bits of meat. I made supper, avoiding the cockroaches and washing every utensil before using it. I sat in the living room. I ate, drank half the bottle, and went to bed at eleven after turning out the lights, closing the interior doors and drawing the deadbolt on the outer door. I woke up at night, thirsty. Hesitantly I walked to the bathroom and the kitchen. I left the light on and kept thinking that the flat was vulnerable to burglars. I slept. I dreamt that a burglar was inside the flat and that I was failing to catch him. I woke up at noon the next day. I took a shower, ate my breakfast and read an article about enlargement of the prostate. I noticed that my heart was beating irregularly and that I was short of breath. I left. I bought a lemon, some flour, some Armenian sesame *halva* and some *morozhenoye* and returned to the *obshchezhitie*. After an hour I saw Vera the Jewish girl in my doorway. Her legs were bare, her skirt short and her hair a frizzy mess. She had come to return a record she had borrowed. She asked about Hans.

I asked her in turn, my eyes on her naked thighs, 'Aren't you cold?'

'On the contrary, I'm hot.'

108

I received a postcard from Nadezhda and her husband. I put it on the desk next to the newspapers I was working on. There was a knock, and I opened the door for Anastasia. She noticed the postcard and asked, 'Is that from your friend who was here a few days ago?'

'Yes, how did you know?'

She ignored the question but asked, 'Where's Hans?'

'I don't know.'

'Impossible—you guys are close like this.' She lifted two fingers together.

Hans came after she left. I told him what Anastasia had said. He said, 'I told her I wanted to break up, and she made me promise to stay with her until the end of the year. I agreed. Just the end of the year, and from the first day of the New Year—I'll be free.'

'She's a delicate person.'

'She doesn't turn me on any more.'

109

I thought of getting Nadia a present for the Christmas holidays. Would it be appropriate to give her the paper underpants, or some imported soap and a bottle of perfume? I offered her the panties. She said, 'I don't accept presents. I don't want to feel I owe anyone anything.' 'You don't have to feel you owe me anything,' I assured her. She took the panties and shook my hand, then noticed she had locked her key inside her office. A guy with a moustache went to find her a key. An Egyptian visitor arrived, apparently a top government official in Egypt, led by Lotfi. We introduced ourselves just as two students appeared, an Egyptian and a Syrian. The Syrian sprang up to accompany the visitor and started walking beside him. I heard the Egyptian say quietly to Lotfi, 'No, you should guide him—don't let that guy steal him from you.'

I returned to Nadia, stepping aside for a blonde who was coming out of her office. Nadia followed her with her eyes, saying to me, 'You know, this is a colleague of ours who is Jewish and wants to emigrate to Israel, and we asked her, "How could you turn your back on the country that fed you, educated you?"' I saw the panties lying on the desk, unwrapped.

'How's the *nastroyenie*?' she asked me.

'Lousy.'

'Go down south.'

'Alone?'

'Take your countrywomen along.'

'Where are you spending Christmas Eve?'

'I don't know.'

'Come over to our place.'

Just then a student walked in; she didn't answer. But she kept moving around. Jumping up. Sitting down. Tugging at her sweater. She got up to go to the window, and her trousers creased up between her legs. She put her hand over the cleft. She showed me a black shoe with a 7-inch heel.

'Where did you get that?' I asked.

'*Na rynke*. Do you like them?'

'Not bad.'

She didn't like my answer and said, 'Do you know how much they cost? 200 roubles. But yesterday it was 220!'

Her officemate came in. They started talking about shoes. She noticed the panties and pointed to them, saying, 'Get those things out of here!' Nadia paid no attention. Various people entered the room and I kept expecting one of them to see the panties and comment.

She didn't care, and no one said anything. I was sitting close to her, so I leant over and whispered, 'Why don't you put this scandal away?'

She snapped, 'We consider this something natural.'

I didn't understand what she meant.

The phone rang; Nadia answered. Suddenly, she started crying. She said, 'My mom has heart trouble, and they say it's because of me.' A little later she added that she had promised her mom a visit, but she had stayed too late at a girlfriend's house and ended up sleeping over. Her mother had collapsed when she had told her that she was divorcing the guy she had married just a few days earlier—she didn't know why she had done so, since she didn't love him—she had known another guy for four years and got angry at him for some trivial thing and decided to marry someone else.

'How are you able to sleep with him if you don't love him?' I said.

'I don't. I sleep in the next room.' She started tidying her desk drawers and told a long story about the noise in modern blocks of flats, how you could hear the noise from the floors above and below.

I said, 'That explains why you don't sleep with your husband.'

'How?'

'You don't want anyone to hear you.'

'If I like someone, I sleep with him—no problem.'

A young man came in, the same guy who had brought her the key at the Institute gate. She told him, 'Mama is unwell and they've taken her to the hospital —she needs a visit and some flowers.' She stepped out of the room and I heard him say, 'Shit.' She came back and asked him, 'Why don't you say anything?' Then she stood up and asked me, 'Could I have a cigarette, please?' I gave her one and went to light it but she said, 'No, I've got my matches.' I stood up to leave; she signalled me with her eyes to stay. She left the room briefly but returned a moment later. She told her colleague, 'Someone is going to call shortly—tell him I've gone to see my mother.' She picked up her purse and a bulging plastic bag and got ready to leave.

'You didn't answer me—are you spending Christmas with us?' I persisted.

'I don't know, we'll talk tomorrow.'

'You'll be here in the morning?'

'Of course.'

110

In the morning I went to the Institute. It was warm outside. The snow had stopped. I walked fast and felt my heartbeat speed up. I found her in the office with her officemate, and she told me her mom was back home and everything was in order. I sat down to wait until we were alone. The officemate didn't budge. Nadia left the room and came back clapping with joy, 'We're going now.' She was speaking into the phone.

I asked her again, 'So are you coming to our place?'

'You guys have your party.'

'I'll be waiting for you.'

'I'll be at the *obshchezhitie* visiting the second-year students. I can drop by and see you guys after midnight.'

'What about tomorrow?' I pursued. 'I've got used to seeing you every day now.'

'When? You know I have a husband and a mother.'

'In the daytime. At night, I'll leave you to your husband.'

'*Ladno*, I'll be at my mom's place from II to 5, call me there.' She gave me the number and said, 'But don't tell any of the other students.'

'Of course not.'

I left the Institute with Hans. I recounted my conversation with Nadia and told him I was considering making a restaurant reservation for the next day.

'You won't find one. No restaurant is taking reservations now.'

'Then I'll take her to Abdel Hakim's flat.'

He said she was the type that gives it up on the first date; he always lost interest if a girl didn't.

'How do you know that about her?' I asked.

'I used visit her house every morning after her mom went out.'

We bought two bottles of vodka and stood in a long line for oranges. I pictured Nadia in front of me in a bikini with her white legs and her hair hanging down on her face. He said, 'There are two kinds of men—like Tadros, he's flagrantly masculine. But you and me, we're more a mixture of masculine and feminine. The typical woman is passive. She enjoys being pursued, and a numb ecstasy spreads through her body right on the verge of giving in.'

I said, 'I need a little time to get to know a woman before I can sleep with her.'

111

I slept badly, uneasy as a teenager before his first date. I shaved, ate breakfast and put on my best clothes and new shoes. Hans gave me directions to the Berezka to buy liver and tripe and other stuff. I took along some *certifikati*, the paper roubles that stood in for dollars. I went out sluggishly. I got the bus to the metro station, then the metro to Kievskaya. Then a crowded trolleybus to Marx Prospect, then another trolleybus. I walked for a long time looking for the Berezka. At 1 p.m. I called her mom, who said she hadn't come or promised to. I crossed the street several times looking for the shop; no use. At three, I called again. Her sister answered: she had called and would be over in a little while. I decided to move fast. For half an hour I stood in line at a butcher shop ready to buy roast beef—but when I got up to the counter, the salesman announced they were out. I decided not to buy a roast duck instead. I continued the hunt for the Berezka. I stood in front of a telephone booth waiting for a fat old lady who spoke very slowly. After she got off the phone she stood there staring at me in silence. I realized that she was waiting for me to help get her out of the booth. I managed it somehow, got her across the street, then came back to make the call. Her mom said she had come, then gone out again and would be back that evening around nine. By chance I stumbled on the shop. Many goods were available, well-organized and attractively displayed—expensive furs, Finnish fish, Dutch cheese, Arab fruits, almond candy, tomatoes and canned fish from Bulgaria, Dutch chicken wrapped in shiny cellophane, Marlboro cigarettes, in addition to some Russian products not available in regular stores. I bought a lamb liver, two lemons, a wrapped cucumber, salmon, some Danish cheese and Finnish vodka. I returned to the *obshchezhitie*. Hans was waiting for me. We fried the liver and drank the vodka.

Anastasia joined us, complaining, 'Why didn't you invite me? I was sitting there waiting.'

'Tomorrow is the last day of our relationship.' he reminded her.

'It doesn't matter.' After a moment, she said, 'In my city there's no meat and we have to buy it on the black market.'

'Why do people put up with that?' I asked.

'They taught us not to protest. If I say anything, I'll go to prison.'

She mentioned that her Italian roommate had rented a hotel room with the Yugoslav guy so she—that is, Anastasia—now had the place to herself. She invited Hans up to her room. I decided not to call Nadia.

112

At 9 a.m. I felt Hans enter the room with Anastasia, put on his overcoat and leave. I got up and had breakfast. I put on Rossini, then Carmen and the Bolero. I picked up the familiar issue of *Playboy*. I cut out the pictures of the Pharaohs, and pasted them in scandalous sexual positions on the glass door of the wardrobe. I read an article about penis size. A female reader was interviewed saying the size didn't matter as long as the man knew how to use what he had. Anastasia came back with Hans from their walk in the snow. I told them about the reader's opinion. She said there was a Russian saying to the same effect. She noticed the pasted Pharaoh pictures and laughed. I pointed to one of them, saying, 'Ramses II. He married forty women and had over one hundred children.' She suggested we go visit her unmarried friend who told fortunes and could tell us what to expect for the coming year—in the romantic department, anyway. She said, 'I called her this morning and she said she had two girls over and one sleeping guy.' I sensed that she didn't really want to go, and in fact we all decided to stay. I heard Hans tell her, 'I don't want you.' She said, 'Why? There's nothing left for me but to become a *lesbianka*.' Some visitors stopped by:

Hind, and Anar with a Latvian guy. Then Tamara appeared with her fantastic legs and full lips. She exchanged kisses with Hans and danced with him. They gathered around the Pharaoh pictures. The glasses emptied, and then began a hunt for alcohol through all the dorm rooms. Hind said the shops were closed and the only solution now was to ask the taxi drivers who kept bottles of vodka on hand to sell in situations like this. I put on my coat and went down to find a taxi. I got as far as the local cinema and noticed that in half an hour they would be screening a film from West Germany. I bought a ticket and went in. I sat next to a woman who was alone. Gradually I drew my leg closer to hers, waiting to feel her response; then I started to rub against her leg with mine, and at first she let me. Perhaps she didn't notice or she wanted to know what I wanted. And really, what did I want? I moved my leg away.

113

In the afternoon I went to the Institute. I avoided Nadia's office, but I ran into her in another room; she was combing her hair. She was wearing a short blue dress that showed off her splendid legs. She looked radiant and bursting with life. She said, pointing to the armchair next to her, 'Do you want me?'

'I always want you, but not now.' Then I added, 'You're so elegant and pretty. Do you have a party tonight?'

She didn't answer but asked instead, 'How was your party? I bet the *obshchezhitie* was quite a scene.' '*Normal'no*, fine. Is your office open?'

'Do you need to use the phone? Come.' She walked me there. Her officemate was on the phone. Nadia sat down, then stood up and walked over to me and said, '*Skuchno*? Are you bored?' Then she asked the office-mate to get off the phone. I made my call. She fidgeted in circles and then said, 'Let's get out of here.'

'Let's go.'

We went out in the hall. On the landing one of the shy Russian boys gushed, 'Nadia, you look really beautiful today.'

'*Spasibo,*' she smiled, walking away quickly. Then, to me, 'Come, I'll show you around the Institute.'

We went down to the ground floor. We met the old guy who worked in the storeroom, staggering from drink. He called to her, 'Am I needed?'

'Not today, Dima,' she answered, laughing. She told me, 'He was always drunk. He retired two years ago but kept coming to work. We didn't need him most of the time, but this one time we suddenly needed him and couldn't find him, he had got sick of waiting and gone out drinking. He had his pay docked as punishment, and after that he would come every day and glumly ask, "Am I needed?"'

We reached the end of a corridor and she stopped, saying, 'Here's a dark room I discovered.'

'By yourself?'

She burst out laughing. We went back to her office. Why had she taken me to the dark room, what had she wanted?

She picked up a Balzac book and said, 'Part Two. I read Part Three before. It's scary to read it backwards, like you're reading the story of someone's youth and you already know how she died in her old age.'

The telephone rang. She answered and greeted her mother. She looked worried. She moved the receiver away from her face and then brought it back, saying, '*Khorosho, khorosho.*'

It rang again.

She answered quickly, saying, 'Yes, *khorosho*, are you at home? I'll call you.'

I was contemplating her legs the whole time and noticed that she didn't raise her eyes from them either.

I left her office and stood with Dima the drunk employee outside. He complained about his teenage children, calling them *hooligany* who didn't care about school but only about American rock music. I left the Institute and walked, hunched over, to the *obshchezhitie*. I found Lotfi's room open. Fuad the Circassian from Syria was sitting next to him with tears flowing down his cheeks. He made me sit down next to him. I asked him harshly, 'Are you drunk?' Hamid and Bashar showed up. Fuad exploded at Hamid, 'You think I'm crude? Who do you think you are? I'll walk all over you and Moshe Dayan, too. I just got a letter that my brother's been killed in the war.' He vomited. I picked up a rag by the door and wiped it clean. He wanted to hit me when I started joking with him. Lotfi and I stepped out into the hall for a smoke. A girl walked by—plump and sallow. She smiled at us. Lotfi winked at me and said in a proud whisper, 'Do you know Marsha? I've slept with her. She was fun.'

114

I had barely finished cleaning and tidying up the room when someone knocked on the door. I opened it to find the *komendantsha* and several elderly men and women. I recognized one of them: the head of the health committee. The *komendantsha* said they were inspecting the rooms for cleanliness and insisted on coming in. I stepped aside for them. They stood in the middle of the room looking peering in all directions. The *komendantsha* walked up to the wardrobe and stood staring at the Pharaoh pictures. She opened her mouth to say something; it stayed open. Then she ordered, 'Remove those pictures at once.'

115

Hans got dressed and prepared to go out. There was a knock. I opened the door and saw Zoya. She looked glum; her clothes hid her belly. Hans greeted her coldly and excused himself. She took off her overcoat and scarf, revealing a floral skirt and a low-cut sweater. Grimly she sat down on the edge of the bed next to me and asked, 'Do you have anything to drink?' I opened a bottle of wine for her. I looked at her belly and said, 'What have you done?' She said, 'What all women do.' I opened my arms, and she buried her head in my chest. In that position I could see her full breasts—enlarged by the pregnancy, it seemed. I put my hand inside her sweater and held one of them. At that moment there was a knock and Hans came back in looking for something. She jumped up and grabbed her shawl and coat, saying, 'I have to go now, my mom's waiting.'

116

The dean for foreign students called me in. He was tall and sturdily built, with greying hair, rumoured to be KGB. He welcomed me and took me to a corner of his office, where we sat at a small table. He said, smiling, 'What's up with those pictures? From what I hear, you guys don't need them.'

'It was just an attempt to shake up the old revered images and see them from a contemporary perspective.'

'And what about those newspapers you've been cutting up?'

'It's part of my history research.'

'It's just the two of you in the room now.' His blue eyes drilled into me. I flushed.

'No, four.'

'Hamid and Farid are staying somewhere else.'

'Sometimes.'

He asked me about the situation in Egypt. The meeting ended. I went out wondering what it meant. Was it a message that he knew everything about me? And where was he getting it? I thought of everyone who had stopped by the room. It could be any one of them. I reported the whole conversation to Hans and asked what he thought. He didn't comment.

117

Nadia asked, 'Where are we going? I hope it's not the *obshchezhitie*—the students know me.' I said, 'Don't worry, it's a friend's flat.' Not a single muscle twitched on her face. I thought of how little she knew about me. She couldn't even pronounce my name right. She was wearing a wool hat and a matching scarf. She followed me into the flat and sat down on the sofa in the living room. I had prepared a feast, but she didn't eat anything, only drank a little vodka. She didn't mind that there was no music. She wouldn't stop chattering. She asked me about Hans, whether he ever came to this flat.

'Sometimes.'

'Alone?' Then without waiting for an answer she told me about a handsome Afghan guy who had been in love with her and sent her letters.

'Did you sleep with him?'

'There wasn't time.'

'Did you love him?'

'How could I? He was married.'

Then she asked me, as though hesitating or trying to make the tone of her question as distant as possible from what was on her mind, 'How much time do you have left at the Institute? And are you going straight back to your country afterwards?'

'I don't know yet.'

'And what about Hans?'

'Same with him.'

She seemed to fall into a reverie. She said she had got married to get away from her mother who always wanted her home by midnight, and that her husband was from the Baltic. She didn't love him, she repeated. I said, 'Maybe he's just in it for the residence permit.' She had thought of that before, but, 'No, I think he actually has no desire to live in Moscow.'

'Well, maybe he was in love with you.'

'That's what I think.'

Her body took on a receptive posture, with no corresponding gesture from my side. She raised her glass and I did the same. She linked her arm through mine and kissed me, saying, 'Now everything is by the rules.'

I realized I would get her that night. But I had to be careful; she could still change her mind at the last minute. I told her I liked when her hair was loose around her face. She helped me take out the hairpins. I hugged her hard. She pressed her thigh against me to feel my response. But it wasn't there. I said in an intense voice, as if trying to convince myself, 'I want you so bad.'

'*Khorosho,*' she said right away. I wanted to take off her boots, but she stopped me: '*Ya sama*, I'll do it. Where's the bathroom?'

I turned out the lights. She came back in a little while and undressed shyly. She wouldn't let me watch or come close until she was under the sheet. Her perspiration smelt odd, and there was an odour coming from her feet, too. Unwashed socks? I was tipsy enough to ignore the smell business. Her body was soft. Breasts unexpectedly full like pears. Her lips were dry; she moistened them with her tongue when I kissed her. Any touch to her ear made her laugh. Her head kept moving around. I bent down over her and she opened her legs. She bent her knees a little, but I couldn't manage to get inside. I was terrified. Where was the place? Had I forgotten? Or maybe I had never known. All the flesh around her vagina was confusing. I managed to enter, but not all the way. Her face looked up at me. Even in the dark I could see she was confused and scared. I lost my erection. I lay down next to her. I cupped her breast in my hand, enjoying the softness of the curve joining it to her chest. I wanted to kiss her stomach, but she wouldn't let me. I went to go down on her, but she pulled away sharply. She allowed me her legs, having first slammed them nervously closed and arranged them in the most beautiful pose, raising her head to stare down at them.

I put my thigh between her legs and felt her hot and wet above my knee. I moved my knee, but she didn't respond. This woman didn't waste her time on adolescent games. I moved into position above her again, hoping she would hold me and kiss me and fondle me and tell me that everything would be fine, that I was the greatest man in the world. And at that moment I became a little boy on his mother's bosom, even though I was at least ten years older than her. But the moment passed. My impotence returned. She said, trying to take my mind off it, that her officemate was very taken with me, that she was forty-six and had lived for twenty years in a flat where her ex-husband lived in one room and his mistress in another room, and she couldn't have children because of a bad abortion, and she kept wishing some young twenty-seven-year-old guy would fall in love with her and want to marry her. I asked about her other officemate. She said, 'Sveta? She can't keep anything to herself. She even confessed to me all about how she had slept with her own little brother a while back.' Nadia said she had met Galia, Adnan's girlfriend, who had told her to call if she ever needed any clothes, and that once the assistant director had asked her to look around for some shoes for his fiancée, and Galia had brought some for 200 roubles. I pulled her towards me; she resisted. I thought this show of resistance must be meant to arouse me. But it didn't happen. I said, 'I'm afraid of you, that's why.' Rubbing against the rough sofa upholstery was starting to hurt my knees. But she showed no sign of boredom or annoyance. When she realized the situation would not change, she said calmly. 'What time is it? I have to go. You're tired today.' I didn't try to stop her. She drank a glass of water and we got dressed. In the taxi she asked me, 'Why are you down?' I said, 'Sorry for what happened.' She pressed herself against me, put her head on my shoulder and fell asleep.

118

I went to her office at the Institute. She was wearing a red dress slit above the knee. She felt my eyes moving towards the slit and put a bashful hand over it. I asked her, 'What are you doing tomorrow?'

'I don't know.'

'Let's meet.'

'Some other time—I have to stop by my mom's in the morning, then at two I have to pick up a dog and bring it home.'

'At five, then.'

'Where?'

'At the same station.'

'So I have to get on the Circle Line again,' she said, annoyed.

Her officemate walked in, shouting, 'A goose! What a goose I've found! An hour and a half I queued for it.'

'Where?' asked Nadia eagerly.

'A shop nearby—want to come with me? I'll stop back in and maybe score something else, maybe some fruit, we'll buy a lot and put it in the window so it doesn't rot.'

Nadia frowned, 'If they have bananas or tangerines or Finnish eggs or Dutch chicken today, then why not every day? Why do they only dump food on us right before holidays—and in miserly quantities so people have to stand in line for hours?'

Hans appeared at the office door. He looked at me coldly. Nadia said her husband was home now with some of his friends, and she had agreed that Hans would walk her to the bus stop. I left the Institute alone. As I walked by the liquor store, I saw the old custodian Dima inside looking around. He had two fingers on his jacket lapel signalling for two vodka-bottle mates.

119

At noon I headed for Abdel Hakim's flat, tidied up and carefully shaved. I found an open envelope on the dining table. I picked it up. A letter from one of Abdel Hakim's friends. I read:

Please

1 arrange to send the letter for my sister's treatment, preferably translated. I will send you the medical report on the whole situation. For your information: a lump was found in the left breast, and about a week later there was a biopsy that showed it to be cancerous, so they did surgery to remove the whole left breast and the lymph node in the armpit—it had not spread there. She needs an invitation to continue her treatment at the Cancer Institute in Moscow along with her brother and an accompanying doctor.

2 purchase a Riga transistor radio with its 21-volt transformer.

3 buy two face massagers (11 roubles each) from GUM.

4 send ulcer medication for a patient who is dear to me: 4 bottles.

I put the letter back. At five I went out to Kievskaya Station. I stood waiting for her in the entrance. I was cold, hungry and tired, devoid of desire. I thought the fatigue would take my mind off my impotence. She was late; I hoped she wouldn't come: I'd go back, eat a good meal and go to sleep. I went upstairs to the eastbound platform. A sea of people speaking different languages, wearing clothing of various colours and styles, giving off many odours. I stood near four sailors who had sat down near a tea and beer kiosk. Two of them were playing chess. The other two were passing a vodka bottle. One of them said to the other, 'Don't worry, the trains always come on time. It's probably the only thing that works in this country.' A girl walked by wearing a light coat over multicoloured trousers, a yellow shawl over her braided hair. From her features and hairstyle I could tell she was Tajik. There were Uzbek families sitting on big suitcases, and Gypsy women selling beauty supplies. They had brightly coloured skirts and gold earrings that clashed with their dirty faces. One of the drinkers asked me, 'Where from?' I replied, 'An Arab, from Egypt.' One of the Uzbeks heard me and approached, followed by his group. They wore embroidered skullcaps and galabeyas over wide colourful trousers. They looked lost and confused, and one of them was holding an Arabic Quran. I walked towards the exit; they followed me. I stopped; they stopped. I kept walking; so did they. Had they chosen me for their imam?

I went down to the platform. At half past five I decided to leave. I worked myself up against her: a frivolous, stupid, feeble-minded girl. Someone carried a drunk out of the station and put him in an ambulance. At quarter to six she showed up. She said, 'Sorry, I won't be late again.'

Her hair was loose around her face. She wore a leather jacket over a sky-blue blouse and a short blue-green skirt and shiny high-heeled boots up to her knees. She seemed fresh, as through straight from the bath. We went to the flat. She wouldn't eat anything and drank very little. She said, 'Talk to me.' I leant closer to kiss her. She moved her face away. I tried again. She gave me her lips. I got an erection and pressed against her so she could feel it and be reassured! After a brief silence I awkwardly invited her to lie down. I stepped into the other room to get a blanket and pillow to spread on the floor. When I returned, I found her standing by the window in her undershirt; she had turned off the light and taken off her clothes. I spread out the blanket, then undressed and stood next to her. I put my hand on her back and led her to the blanket. I stretched out on it and was surprised at the force filling my body. I moved over on top of her. I tried but could not find the place. The force went away. I said to her accusingly, 'Why did you push me away? You're sneaky.'

'I'm not—you're stupid.'

A moment later she said, 'You think I'm bad.' I kissed her with surprising passion and she moved under me. I bit her lips and said I felt like beating her for coming late. I was looking for that thing, the thing that would turn her on, which would turn me on as well. But her response was ordinary: neither resistance nor any special enthusiasm. I bit her lip a few times. My desire came back. I felt like shouting in Russian—Hurrah! I moved the pillow from under her head because her vagina was set a little bit to the back. I penetrated her as she sighed tepid little sighs. Or maybe they were fake. Her eyes were open wide; maybe it hurt a little, because I wasn't moving in a disciplined rhythm but thrusting like a novice. When she felt me looking at her, she shut her eyes in a show of passion. As I gained confidence, my desire redoubled. I started more slowly; she made no movement or sound in response. She was extremely tight—limited experience? Or had she never been pregnant? I felt the pressure of her flesh around me and almost came, but I stopped moving. I tried a few more times to find her response. Did she take a long time, or climax quickly? I told her, 'I want us to come together.' But I couldn't hold back—I buried my head in her neck and moved. She responded without a quiver. She kissed my upper arm. After a while she pushed me out and got up to go to the toilet. Then she came and lay back down. She asked me about myself, carefully. I asked her about her sexual response.

'Simple and quick—I feel relief,' she said.

'I don't think so.'

'Why?'

'Because you didn't come.'

'That's what you think?'

After half an hour I was surprised to feel aroused again. I asked her to move her perineal muscles, but she didn't understand. I finished suddenly. It wasn't a good performance. Maybe because I still didn't know what aroused her. Or maybe it was the language barrier. Or maybe I was looking for something that didn't exist.

120

Through the windowpane I looked out at the accumulating snow. I said to Hans, 'Remember that Fellini film where the crazy guy climbs the tree and shouts, "I want a woman!"? Now I'm that guy.' I headed for my bed, repeating, 'Come to me, mama.' I lay down and pulled up the covers, saying, 'I'm so tired. You can't even imagine how tired I am.'

121

I saw that Lotfi's door was open and he was sitting there, dressed up, reading a book about aesthetics. I said hello and he invited me in. We sat chatting. I heard quick footsteps in the hall and he jumped up, calling out, 'Marsha.' But the steps continued past the door; some other girl, apparently. He sat down on the bed and said he had totally ended the thing with her. In six days his wife was coming from Egypt. Hamid and Sharif came in. We closed the door carefully and turned on Voice of America. It was scrambled, but we managed to make out some of what it was saying. The leadership in Beijing had declared that Beethoven, Schubert and Mozart were playing tunes out of 'the old capitalist moneybox'. The radio commented that the Chinese had been annoyed by the eager reception given to three Western orchestras the year before and had turned up the attacks on decadent musicians. One of their newspapers had called Beethoven 'a German capitalist' while claiming that Schubert had suffered from depression because he was persecuted by Austria's feudalist rulers—had he been a good Marxist, he would have finished the missing symphony. And Mozart was not even worth talking about, having written nothing that could be compared to *The White-Haired Girl*, the Chinese revolutionary ballet. I laughed as I mentioned having read in an Egyptian newspaper about how a famous Islamist preacher had declared that listening to Beethoven was a sin.

122

Lotfi and I went to Abdel Hakim's place. He had a few Egyptian students over. He mentioned that Heikal had hinted in a recent column that the Israelis wouldn't retreat one step from now on. Lotfi said Sadat was selling the country to the Americans, and that the Egyptian students at Moscow University had posted a wall news-paper with a caricature of Sadat embracing Mimi Shakib, the film star charged with heading a prostitution ring; the caption said: 'Opening up to America.' Some guy I didn't know mentioned that the Egyptian news-papers had published wiretap transcripts of the actresses accused in the case. And that a famous one had said to the chief defendant: 'Him? He's just an old geezer! Send him over, I'll take care of it.' And during the investigation she told the prosecutor: 'You're here keeping tabs on me? Go home and see what your mother and your sister are doing!' The conversation moved on to the state of journalism in Egypt, and Abdel Hakim said that Ali Amin—after he was named to replace Heikal as editor of *Al-Ahram*—wrote to demand that the actresses arrested in the prostitution ring be compensated for reputational damage. And on TV he shouted about his plans for *Al-Ahram*: first get its underwear right, and only then take care of its outer clothes. Shehata said that when the Egyptian students in the philosophy department had organized a discussion on Tawfiq al-Hakim's *The Return of Consciousness*, the attendees had preferred to spend their time playing the dumb childish game of 'Truth or Dare' instead. He said they were all past the age of curiosity and getting excited about ideas; all they cared about now was securing their future, buying a car and a refrigerator, knowing whose palm to grease. Stability. Zaki gave an example of how Egyptian senior officials operated: A delegation from the Egyptian Industrialization Organization came to Moscow for training; at the Cairo airport, they were each given bags of soap powder and sesame paste to hand over on arrival to their Moscow representatives who would sell it on the black market.

123

In the evening I sat down to work. Belmajid came; I made him tea. Then Anastasia and Haydar turned up. After they left, Marsha stopped by, asking about Hans. I invited her in and poured her some tea. She was a little dressed up, wearing a pink tunic over orange trousers that reminded me of death-row inmates' uniforms. I sat down at my table and continued working. She watched me for a moment, then said she also used to love clipping various articles out of newspapers. She still liked to clip items from French newspapers about newly released films. She had a valuable library now; for example, she knew when Marlon Brando had made his film debut. She said she wanted to hear some Bach. I put on the record. She urged me to keep working. I cast a glance over at her and found her crossing one leg over the other. I asked her why she never made eye contact with the person she was talking to but looked instead at his shoulder. She said, 'It makes the task of having a conversation easier for me.' Hind came in, asking about Hans; I served her tea. She said she needed a good proverb to post on the wall in a girls' school. 'Silence is Golden,' I suggested. The two girls left together. Lotfi arrived, somewhat dressed up, and said he'd like some tea. I realized he was looking for Marsha. I told him she was here just a minute ago. He said the whole thing was over as far as he was concerned.

124

I spread the Egyptian newspaper in front of me and noticed a religious paragraph printed in a box in the corner. An episode from the biography of Muhammad: One day the Prophet was exhausted and went into a tent with Abu Bakr al-Siddiq and lay down to sleep with his head in Abu Bakr's lap. A viper came and stung Abu Bakr in the heel but he was afraid to make any movement lest he disturb God's Prophet. But soon the pain overcame him and his eyes filled with tears, one of which fell on the Prophet's face and woke him. He asked: 'O Abu Bakr, what is the matter?' Abu Bakr recounted to him what had happened. Verily, the Prophet lifted his companion's foot and spat some of his holy saliva on it, which was like unto a clear balm, and the swelling subsided with the help of God the Almighty.

This story gave me something to think about. Either it was true, or else it had been concocted to counter widespread tales of Christian miracles. In the first case, it testified either to the Prophet's supernatural powers or to Abu Bakr's faith in those powers. For

miracles are caused by faith. I recalled William the
Englishman: when his mom had cancer, she cured it
through a regimen of yoga.

125

I had known Sami Nashed at university. Under Nasser's rule he was imprisoned on charges of being a Communist. After the 1967 war, he had settled in Beirut. Now I got a call from him: he was in Moscow on an invitation from the Afro-Asian Solidarity Committee. Where? In quarantine! I got the address from the guard and left the *obshchezhitie*. The day started out clear. A foot of new snow gleamed in the sun. The metro was crowded with ice skaters heading outside the city. The streets filled up with crews of snow-clearing women with shovels, women with net bags full of oranges, men with vodka bottles in their pockets and New Year's fir trees clasped in their arms. I took the metro out past the Moscow city limits. After asking for directions a few times, I came to an empty tree-covered spot. I found him in a wide cage surrounded with wire, like in a zoo. He was wearing an elegant suit under a suede overcoat. I burst out laughing, and after a few seconds he joined in. He told me how he had prepared and dressed up for the visit, buying new clothes in hopes of female conquests. Shortly after arrival he had told his Soviet hosts he was suffering from severe diarrhoea, and they had put him in quarantine where he would stay until his departure ten days later. We talked about life in Beirut and Moscow. I told him that if you held real elections here, the Communist party would lose. He was shocked. He said a leftist Lebanese newspaper had claimed that Kissinger had advised Sadat to move troops to the border after the collapse of talks with Israel, which meant that America had given the green light for the Egyptian army to cross the Suez Canal. The same newspaper affirmed that the oil embargo had actually helped the US economy, since the higher oil prices meant billions of petrodollars deposited in American banks. I promised him I would visit again and left him there, fingers wrapped around the wire of his cage. In the metro I stood next to a cheerful old man who held an open bottle of vodka. He smiled at two young men, then lifted the bottle to his lips and recited what seemed to be some lines of verse: 'I'm so bored, I want to get drunk.' A fussy red-faced young man scolded him, 'No bottles in the metro!' The seat in front of me opened up, and I sat down absentmindedly. A standing passenger in her fifties chided me, 'Young man, didn't they teach you in school to respect ladies and offer them a seat?' I stood up, apologizing that I had not noticed her. The lady sat down, looking around to see other passengers' reactions to the little scene. I busied myself staring at the red-granite station as it came into view, decorated with stained glass and crystal chandeliers.

126

The last day of the year. The *obshchezhitie* was quiet. I sat in my room listening to 'Al-Nil Nagashi'. Then we started getting ready for the party. We put three bottles of champagne in the window along with a bottle of Polish vermouth and three bottles of vodka. We put out plates of pickles, cold cuts, smoked fish and pickled herring. An hour before midnight, we heard loud noises coming from Khalifa's room. Anastasia came over, wearing black velvet trousers and a green velvet top. She had laced it tight to hide her fat stomach; she had also done her hair in a special braid and put on heavy make-up. She smelt of French perfume. She had brought each of us a present: a small bottle of cognac wrapped in red ribbon with a little wooden Russian doll. We gave her four boxes of Marlboros, a metal bracelet and some Western chocolate. We exchanged kisses. She said the girls were busy mixing flour with salt, waiting for midnight when each one would drop a shoe from the window, and in the morning they would rush outside and each of them would kiss the first man she met near her shoe and be his love. She looked at Hans and added, 'I didn't join them, because my man is here.' She wrapped her arms around him; he kissed her. She went out and came back with a radio set and a lovely little New Year's tree, which she put on the table on a piece of cloth. We turned out all the lights except the desk lamp.

I went up to Svetlana's room to invite her but was told she was in Prague. I went back to my room, leaving the door open. The three of us opened a bottle of champagne and waited for the end of Brezhnev's speech on the radio. He spoke slowly, stuttering as though he found it hard to get the words out. Then we toasted the New Year. And the ruckus began. A Kazakh guy showed up carrying a bottle of champagne and a glass and insisted that we drink with him, then headed off to knock on the doors of other rooms and pour for the inhabitants. Then we too began forcing anyone who walked by to have a drink with us. Lina stopped by, extending her hand for me to kiss; I used it instead to pull her towards me to kiss her mouth. She averted her face and asked, 'Did you miss me?' 'Of course,' I said. She entered, turned on the light and looked at the table. She put out her hand, quickly grabbed a slice of pickle and a bit of smoked fish and a Marlboro, and left. Down the hall, the drunks started breaking bottles. They danced Cossack style, yelling '*Kalinka, kalinka moya*'. Hind and Kolya came and stood around for a minute looking confused, then left. Hamid and Sharif and their girlfriends turned up, then Bashar came with Helene. I served them champagne, and Hind slow-danced with Hamid. Haydar arrived, then his girl, a Mongolian, came over looking for him. They were followed by Mikha, who was drunk. He embraced Hans and kissed him on the mouth. We went and brought one of the Algerians who was all alone and sad. Anar appeared, wearing a miniskirt and accompanied by a Czech guy; I pulled them inside. I danced with her, and the conversation turned to Hans, who was lost in the embraces of Anastasia. She said he was the most beautiful boy at the Institute. She was silent a moment, then said, 'I'm still a virgin, you know. Imagine! Because I'm waiting for love. There are a hundred guys . . . if I wanted them— you know the tragedy of an Eastern girl like me.' She said she had once spent the night with Hans in his room but departed with her virginity intact.

'If you want him, go get him—he'll break up with Anastasia tomorrow.'

She said she believed the man should be the one to go after the girl.

'Hans is not like that,' I said. 'Any girl can grab him.'

'I know he's a *durak*. A fool.'

When Anastasia left the room, Anar danced with Hans, then they stepped behind the wardrobe. I turned my back to them and stood by the door. I saw Anastasia coming in. I got between her and the doorway and asked if she had seen Nadia. She kissed me on the cheek and said in English—which she spoke only when she was drunk—that she knew I was lonely and wished she could help me but she was no good at plotting and scheming. We entered the room, and she saw Hans and

Anar behind the wardrobe. She sat down for a little while, then asked me to help her get rid of Anar. I asked Anar for a dance. Then Anastasia left the room with Hans. I asked Anar, 'How'd it go?'

'He talked about my lips and my breasts and told me to lie down on the bed—that's not what I want.'

'Your mistake.'

'I know,' she said and then went away, promising to be back soon.

We waited for her to return, the drunk Czech boy and I. Then he suddenly took off, leaving me alone. Marsha came and looked around, apparently searching for Lotfi, then quickly left. I sat by myself in the room in front of the table with the tiny fir tree, staring at the door. My prostate pains returned; then I decided to have some coffee with *morozhenoye*. I took the coffee pot to the kitchen and found Anar there with the handsome Latvian guy. He was telling her about his military service and how he had been part of the Czechoslovakian campaign. And how they had been ordered to hold their fire even though the Germans and Poles were firing like crazy. And how so many Russians had died. Some women had sat down in the path of the Russian tanks, which were approaching fast, and when the driver suddenly noticed the women and swerved right, the tank fell into the river and he and the crew with it and the women hurried to the riverbank to weep over the dead Russians. I left the two of them and returned to my room. After a while Anar came back and lay down on the bed, exposing her thighs. Zoya arrived, preceded by her belly and accompanied by her husband. She declined a drink; soon they left. Everyone started heading out. We went out into the cold street. Neighbourhood women had formed circles and were dancing to an accordion. Some of them were dressed up in carnival costumes. Their folk songs mostly revolved around the male organ, its size, or men's impotence or absence. One of them, staggering drunk, shouted, 'I want a man who's *hot*.'

We went back inside, the din rising from every floor. I sat down to chat with Hamid and Sharif. They asked me how we celebrated New Year in Egypt. Hans came in, tipsy, but we kept on talking. He got upset and said he was going to leave; he was a stranger here, no one wanted to talk to him, everyone just kept speaking Arabic. He added, crying, 'I'm alone—alone!' He gathered some of his things, then threw the room key on the floor and left, slamming the door behind him. Gloom filled us. Sharif went out, leaving Hamid. I invited him to sleep over. About an hour later there was a loud knock; I got up and opened the door. I was surprised to see Hans collapsed in a heap on the threshold, muttering something in German. He was barefoot, his shirt torn and his face stained with blood. We lifted him inside the room, stretched him out on the bed and started to wipe the blood he was covered with. I discovered he was missing his underpants. His whole body was covered with blue bruises. Hamid spread the cover over him, and Hans grabbed his forearm. Hamid kissed him on the cheek, but Hans pulled him closer. Hamid jumped back. Hans fell fast asleep. I went out into the hall and lit a cigarette. Hamid joined me. He said in his Syrian dialect. 'You know what that fag did when I had my face close to his? He tried to stick his tongue in my mouth.' Hamid shook his head in disgust. We walked to the end of the hall, but then we heard loud noises behind us. We ran back to the room. The door was open and some things were strewn beside it. Three big stocky Soviet guys were standing there, screaming. One of them was the head of the student council. Another had Central Asian features. The third looked Cossack. I saw Hans crouched naked in a corner.

The Asian student yelled, 'Arabs! Homos like him! Or else why be friends with him and protect him?' The student-council leader jumped in sternly: 'Shut up, you can't say that.' He turned to us and added, 'They caught Mikha fucking him.'

Together they dragged Hans out to the hall, kicked him towards the stairs, then pushed him so he fell all the way down. They ran down after him. Just before dawn they brought him back, wrapped in a grey blanket. He was completely naked. They put him down on the bed and went out. One of them turned to us and said, 'Maybe this stuff is normal in you people's country, but under the Soviet constitution it's punishable by five years' imprisonment.' I put another blanket over Hans. His eyes were open, ringed by dark blue bruises. I asked

Hamid, 'Shouldn't we call an ambulance or take him to a hospital?' A weak voice came from Hans, 'No, not that, I don't want that.'

Hamid left the room to sleep somewhere else. I took off my clothes and got into bed. Sleep did not come. The grey dawn light pierced the window. I stood up and got dressed: clothes, overcoat, *shapka*, scarf, gloves. I left the *obshchezhitie*. The snow was falling thick and fast. It covered everything with white, even the trees. It started to accumulate on my overcoat, my hat and my eyebrows. My fingers and toes began to freeze. Where to go? I turned around, heading back towards the *obshchezhitie*.

Heliopolis
December 2010

Page 32 Sonallah Ibrahim refers to his earlier novel *Amrikanli* (Cairo: Dar al-Mustaqbal al-'Arabi, 2004), whose title can mean both 'American' and 'I Was Master of My Affairs'. It follows the protagonist Shukri as he spends a period in the San Francisco Bay Area teaching at the University of California, Berkeley. *Amrikanli* forms a loose trilogy along with *Ice* and *al-Qanun al-fransi* [The Napoleonic Code] (Cairo: Dar al-Mustaqbal al-'Arabi, 2008).

Page 60 Vladimir Vysotsky, 'Pro Seryezhku Fomina' [About Little Serezha Fomin] (1964). For lyrics in Russian, see https://bit.ly/2WYID9c (last accessed on 30 June 2019).

Page 60 Vladimir Vysotsky, 'Zeka Vasiliev I Petrov Zeka' [Prisoners Vasiliev and Petrov] (1962). For lyrics in Russian, see https://bit.ly/2IBeNyO (last accessed on 30 June 2019).

Page 62 Thornton Wilder, *The Ides of March* (New York: Harper Brothers, 1948), p 79.

Page 79 See entries for November 7–9 in Yousef Khatib, *Palestine Diary* (Damascus: Palestine Publications House, 1971).

Page 108 These poems by Yevgeny Yevtushenko, including 'Keys of the Comandante' quoted in this volume, appeared in *Literaturnaya Gazeta* (8 September 1971).

Page 137 Vladimir Mayakovsky, 'My Soviet Passport' (Herbert Marshall trans.) *Sputnik* 12 (1982). Available online at https://bit.ly/2FwIOhk (last accessed on 1 May 2019).

Page 155 Wilder, *Ides of March*, p. 79.

Page 164 Yevgeny Yevtushenko, 'Keys of the Comandante' in *Che in Verse* (Gavin O'Toole and Georgina Jiménez eds and Albert C. Todd and James Ragan trans) (London: Aflame Books, 2007), pp. 231–3.

Page 175 Tawfiq al-Hakim, *The Return of Consciousness* (Bayly Winder trans) (New York: New York University Press, 1985), p. 28.

Page 216 Norman Lewis, *The Volcanoes Above Us* (London: Jonathan Cape, 1957), p. 104.

In Arabic the word for 'literature' is *adab*, which also carries the meaning of 'polite manners' or 'etiquette'. When Sonallah Ibrahim debuted with the terse 1966 novella *That Smell* (English translation by Robyn Creswell was published in 2013), it struck Arab critics as an insult or an assault against *adab*. His deliberately unornamented style and indecorous themes, from masturbation and flatulence to state surveillance and the marginalization of political prisoners, shoved away established literary forms to expose the hypocrisies of Egyptian society in the so-called golden age of Gamal Abdel Nasser's regime.

Published on 25 January 2011, *Ice* is set in Moscow but employs the alienation effects developed 'at home' forty-five years earlier. The narrator is Shukri, the wry historian familiar to readers of Ibrahim's earlier novels *Amrikanli* (2004) and *al-Qanun al-fransi* (2008). However, the post-traumatic narrator of *That Smell* haunts the story too. The narration presents a numbly factual sequence of events without logical subordination, analysis or even a personal response. The narrator is reduced to a pair of eyes or, more precisely, to a camera, recording impressions to be developed later. While rejecting any claim to understand the people or events described, the narrative foregrounds Shukri's sense of estrangement, pointlessness and anticlimax. The reader, too, gropes for orientation. Friendships and love relationships are tenuous. Situations are ambiguous. All the drama is between the lines.

A few Arab critics have responded indignantly to the slippery surface of *Ice*—reading it as a soulless parade of drunken escapades—and overlooked the yearning for meaningful human connection beneath. However, frozen waters run deep. In his memoir, the Syrian filmmaker Mohamad Malas writes about his friendship with Ibrahim when they shared a dorm room in Moscow, emphasizing how Ibrahim's prison memories shaped his experience.[1] That post-prison perspective underscores the Arab dysfunction glimpsed from a critical distance in *Ice*: the persecution of communists in Egypt and Iraq; the collapse of the Palestinian national movement; President Sadat's neoliberal opening and sudden overtures to the West; Egypt's uninspiring victory in the 1973 war.

Alas, the Red Mecca of socialism offers no redeeming cure. In Elliott Colla's words:

> The setting of Moscow in 1973 is also not incidental, since Ibrahim uses the moment—the

---

[1] Mohamad Malas, 'Portrait of a Friend: Sonallah Ibrahim' (Margaret Litvin trans.), *ALIF: A Journal of Comparative Poetics* 36 (2016): 201–25.

onset of the famous 'Era of Stagnation' in Soviet history—to comment on the gaps between promises and realities of Moscow, that capital city of modern revolution ... But most of all, 1973 has a special resonance for Egyptian Leftists too and in the end, it is this Egyptian meaning that consumes Shukri.[2]

In translating this deceptively flat narrative, I have resisted the urge to insert conjunctions, explanations or indications of logical subordination or motive. In many cases I have rendered the Arabic conjunction ف ('fa') —which can be translated as 'and', 'so', 'then', 'therefore' or even 'but'—with just a semicolon. Many of Ibrahim's paragraphs are very long, spanning several locations and sometimes taking up a whole chapter. While I have occasionally inserted a break to highlight an irony or disjunction not otherwise clear to the English reader, most of the long paragraphs have been preserved. Although I have set off dialogues using quotation marks and new lines, I have striven to keep the claustrophobic stream-of-consciousness effect of the original.

As a novel about being strangers in a strange land, *Ice* contains two sets of cultural references, which I have

[2] Elliott Colla, 'Revolution on Ice', *Jadaliyya* (6 January 2004). Available at: https://bit.ly/324MiBk (last accessed on 26 June 2019).

treated differently. For Arabic terms relating to matters like clothing, food, music, literature, religion or politics, I have tried to domesticate the text, conveying the meaning without notes, stealth glosses or italics (for example, 'stuffed cabbage' instead of '*makdous*') except in some instances where there are non-Arabs in the scene. For Russian and Soviet terms, by contrast, I have used nearly the same level of conspicuous translitera-tion, italics and explanation as in the Arabic original. These strategies aim to replicate the experience of the novel's original intended reader, who would find the Russian cultural references exotic but the Egyptian ones familiar. Indeed, there is a guidebook style to Ibrahim's narrative; the Russian words are boldfaced and defined. The text also exoticizes certain dialect terms used by the narrator's Syrian or Iraqi acquain-tances, a practice I have followed. Where Anglophone readers are likely to know Russian terms or Soviet realia (like Kirgizia or KGB), I have reduced the glossing. I have italicized a few words that the original gives in English.

Shukri spends a lot of his time reading. Whenever pos-sible, I have quoted and cited from existing English translations of the works Ibrahim refers to as well as, of course, the original English publications. Where translations are not available, I have rendered directly from the Arabic and cited the original sources. They are sometimes quoted 'off-label': for example, from the

British historical novel about socialist revolution in Guatemala, Norman Lewis' *The Volcanoes Above Us* (1957)—which reportedly sold 6 million copies in the USSR—the narrator only cites a passage on female sexual narcissism.

*

I am grateful to Hosam Aboul-Ela for midwifing this translation, and to Sayoni Ghosh at Seagull Books for meticulously helping me clarify what is so special about this book. Paul Starkey read the whole manuscript, catching some errors and Americanisms. I also thank Richard Jacquemond for our correspondence while he worked on his French translation (Actes Sud, 2015). Above all, I am grateful for the friendship and help of Sonallah Ibrahim who patiently shared his extensive archive, answered my questions and provoked many new ones.